She intrigued him....

He wondered why she didn't saunter up to the statue of Juliet the way her friend did, touch the bronze arm and wish for love.

Her friend was halfway down the alley, but still the woman lingered, studying the statue with obvious misgivings. He noticed the loose drape of her shirt over her breasts. He noticed the way her teeth caught her full lower lip and worried it.

She inched closer to the statue, then inhaled and touched it. He felt a shock deep inside him, something fierce and jolting, almost painful. She flinched and drew her hand back abruptly, as if the statue had singed her.

Her eyes met his. Through the lengthening shadows, through overgrown vines and the throngs of tourists, he stared into the brightest, most beautiful eyes he had ever seen and discovered that he was unable to breathe, unable to move or think.

He had to follow her. Had to catch her, talk to her, gaze into those mesmerizing eyes once more.

But first, he had to touch the statue....

Dear Reader,

Some books come more easily than others. With some, each and every word must be wrenched painfully out of my heart. With others, the words flow freely. On rare occasion, magic happens: a book seems to write itself. This is one of those books.

In the spring of 1992 my Italian publisher, Edizione Harlequin Mondadori, invited me to be the guest of honor at a readers' party in Verona, Italy.

Verona is haunted by its magnificent heroine, Juliet Capulet. Historians will tell you that Romeo's family actually resided in the neighboring village of Montecchio. (Say Montecchio quickly and it sounds like Montague.) Verona, however, belongs to Juliet.

Each year thousands visit her tomb and leave letters requesting her help in romance. Her statue stands in the courtyard where the famous balcony scene occurred, and legend has it that touching the statue will bring luck in love. Those who touch her statue leave full of joy and hope.

Romeo and Juliet experienced that joy and hope for a tragically brief time. They were so young, so in love. Why couldn't they have lived long enough to teach the world that true love can conquer all? But their spirits do survive—in Verona and in this book.

I'm not sure why *Just Like Romeo and Juliet* seemed to write itself. Maybe it was Verona, the home of the world's greatest love story. Maybe it was Romeo and Juliet themselves, whispering their dreams to me. Maybe it was magic.

Judith Arnold

JUDITH ARNOLD

JUST LIKE ROMEO AND JULIET

Harlequin Books

TORONTO • NEW YORK • LONDON
AMSTERDAM • PARIS • SYDNEY • HAMBURG
STOCKHOLM • ATHENS • TOKYO • MILAN
MADRID • WARSAW • BUDAPEST • AUCKLAND

Published April 1993

ISBN 0-373-16482-3

JUST LIKE ROMEO AND JULIET

Prologue

Juliet was sad.

As always, she glowed; as always, she was his light, his sun, the radiance of his world. Yet he sensed her sadness, the strange melancholia that descended upon her at times, veiling the joy of an eternity spent with a man who loved her more than life itself.

"Precious wife," he murmured, "what troubles you?"

"Ah, my lord." She sighed, a deep, mournful breath, whispering like a breeze down onto the earth. "I long for a happy ending."

"We have our happy ending," he argued. "We are together forever."

"Forever was purchased with our lives, dear Romeo," she lamented. "Love should not end in death. It should bring life. It should lead clashing armies to lay down their swords and embrace one another. It should overcome strife and celebrate peace."

"It should," he agreed, "and sometimes it does."

"Not often enough. I want to create a happy ending."

He gazed down upon the courtyard where a statue of his fourteen-year-old bride still stood, below the balcony where he had laid bare his heart so many years ago. In the late afternoon light of Verona, shadows circled the small, square piazza. May's sweet roses climbed the walls, blooming pink and red. Several women were gathered on the balcony, waving down to a man who stood in the yard, aiming a camera at them.

Romeo's attention returned to the statue of his beloved Juliet. In life she had been more beautiful—and was more beautiful still in death. The statue was mere bronze, graceful and goddess-like, yet cold, except for the highly polished sheen of her right arm and her right breast. Pilgrims and tourists came from all over the world to touch the statue. It was said that if you touched it Juliet would bring you luck in love.

Romeo knew how hard she labored to bring love to the heartsick damsels who caressed the statue's arm and the lonely swains who cupped its bosom. Denied her own happy ending in life, Juliet had made it her mission to bring happy endings to other lovers.

Not only did people come to touch the statue, but they left messages for Juliet at her tomb, tearful notes of woe, beseechments for aid in their romantic ventures. Juliet guided them as best she could; she sent her counsel down in the way only spirits can, imbuing her supplicants with the courage they needed to face love and all its wonders.

Sometimes it seemed too great a burden for her. Sometimes she felt her efforts were not enough. People still battled, still clashed. The world still teemed with strife and sorrow.

"You've brought blessings of love to many," he reminded her.

"It is easy enough to bless two lovers who would have found love in any case," she explained. "The true test of love is to bless those who would never have found love, whose love might be tested as ours was. I want to create a love that can triumph over whatever fate places in its path. I want a happy ending.''

She watched the courtyard, and Romeo watched her. After a minute he discerned a change in her, a sudden alertness as she found what she was looking for in the scene below.

A woman. And a man.

Juliet smiled.

Chapter One

Gillian stared at the weathered balcony protruding from the stone wall. "That's it?"

"The one and only," Nancy confirmed, skimming the page of her guidebook.

Gillian shook her head. "That can't be the real balcony. In the play, didn't Romeo have to climb through an orchard before he reached Juliet's window?" She surveyed the rectangular courtyard, which was surrounded by old, high walls of brick and stone, planted with rose bushes and ivy. "This is *not* an orchard."

"Maybe four hundred years ago it was." Nancy lowered the guidebook and scrutinized the balcony. Gillian could see her friend's eyes growing misty as a wave of cloying romanticism swamped her. *"O Romeo, Romeo! wherefore art thou Romeo?"* she emoted.

"Give me a break." Gillian was as prosaic as Nancy was poetic. For Gillian, the appeal of this excursion to Verona lay in the city's historical sites, its magnificent architecture, its public artwork dating back to the Renaissance and even earlier. When Nancy had suggested that they spend a couple of days in Verona, en route from Milan to Venice, Gillian had been all for it.

Of course, Nancy's concept of Verona had centered exclusively on *Romeo and Juliet*. She and Gillian had already trekked through town to look at the building that allegedly housed Juliet's tomb, and now they were in the presence of what the guidebook asserted was *the* balcony, from the immortal balcony scene during which Romeo and Juliet declared their love for each other.

Maybe the balcony would have looked more authentic if a gaggle of middle-aged British matrons hadn't been leaning over its carved wooden railing, shouting down to a mousy gentleman armed with a camera, "Bertrand, ducky! Make sure you fit all of us into the shot!"

Somehow, Gillian doubted that anything could make this buzzing tourist mecca seem authentic. The entire setting was unbearably hokey—not just the balcony, but the bronze statue of Juliet, which had been rubbed to a high gloss on one arm and, rather obscenely, on one breast. "It says in the guidebook," Nancy reported, "that if you touch the statue, you'll have luck in your next love affair."

"Look where she's been touched," Gillian pointed out, squinting as the sun glared against the statue's gleaming breast.

"It is kind of tacky," Nancy allowed. "But you know men—any opportunity to cop a feel, they'll do it."

"If that's the way men are, why in the world would I want to have a love affair?"

"After three years in the salt mines, Gillian, that's exactly what we both need. Love affairs. Grand passion. Great sex."

What Gillian really needed was rest and recreation, which was precisely the point of this two-week trip to Italy. She and Nancy had just finished their final grueling year of law school. They both had jobs waiting for them back in the States, Nancy with the Wall Street law firm where she'd interned the previous two summers and Gillian with a state labor council in New Jersey. Nancy would be making tons more money than Gillian, which was probably why she'd insisted that they stay at the ritziest, glitziest hotel in Verona. But although she would be earning a modest salary, Gillian would be doing work that meant something to her. She would be fighting for the rights of people like her father and his father before him, union members who toiled hard, who kept the nation functioning and deserved their slice of the pie.

The job would be challenging, and Gillian would spend the next decade or so paying off her educational loans. But before that, she had given herself a special graduation present: a vacation in Italy. Nancy had convinced her they'd earned it. And heaven knew when she'd have the chance to go again.

"There's magic in this courtyard," Nancy intoned, surveying the area, which was swarming with tourists armed with guidebooks similar to hers. "There's love in the air."

"There's rocks in your head," Gillian countered. "Let's go see the Arena."

"I don't know why you want to look at a crumbling old amphitheater when you could be looking at the setting where the greatest love story of all time played itself out. I'm going to touch the statue. Take a picture of me, okay?"

Gillian obligingly took the camera, then waited while several other tourists posed for pictures with the Juliet statue. Finally it was Nancy's turn and Gillian snapped the picture.

"You're better looking than Juliet," she said as she handed the camera back to Nancy.

"Yeah? If the picture proves it, I'm going to hang a framed enlargement in my office. I want clients to walk in and say, 'It is the east, and Nancy is the sun.'"

"I thought your office was on the west end of the building."

"In the shadow of the Twin Towers. I'll be the only sun in the place. Anyway, I touched the statue and I'm ready for love."

"Swell."

"I think you should touch it, too, Gillian. I'd hate for me to be having a splendiferous affair while you were all by your lonesome."

"Thanks for caring," Gillian muttered. "Okay, I'll touch the damned statue. But then we're going to the Arena."

"Forget the Arena—let's go shopping."

"Shopping? Given the room rate at the Leon D'Oro, I'll be lucky if I can afford a cup of espresso for supper."

"Oh, come on. Shop with me. I want to blow a million lire on those green suede boots I saw in that boutique near the Piazza Erbe."

"Why don't you go shopping while I go to the Arena?"

Nancy conceded with a shrug. "Okay. We'll meet back at the hotel at six-thirty."

"Six-thirty. Fine." Gillian glanced toward the arched entry to the street. "The Arena was to the right?"

"You'll find it. First touch the statue," Nancy ordered her.

"Nance—"

"Touch it. Go ahead. It won't bite."

"Of course it won't bite. Juliet specialized in poison and daggers."

Nancy planted her hands on her hips. "Touch it!"

With a sigh, Gillian turned and marched to the statue. The scent of blossoming roses tickled her nostrils; the late afternoon sunshine cast an eerie pink light onto the timeworn stones of the wall. The statue's face was as blank and ageless as bronze could be, her gown nondescript, her demeanor anything but romantic.

Gillian had no reason to hesitate, but she did. It wasn't that she believed touching a statue would bring her luck in love. Nor that she was against a happy affair, if the legend happened to be true. It was just...

She was scared.

Gillian prided herself on her fearlessness, her determination, her sensibility. She abhorred superstition. Yet, in some undefined way, standing in Juliet's long lavender shadow sent a ripple of fear down her spine.

Nancy's voice reached her from across the courtyard, cutting through the din of multilingual chatter. "Go ahead! What have you got to lose?"

Taking a deep breath, Gillian reached out and touched the statue.

HE HAD NOWHERE TO GO, or he would have gone by now. Indeed, he had no idea why he was hanging out at this tourist trap, except that the roses were in flower and he wasn't ready to go back to the flat yet.

Things weren't good with Rosalie. He knew it, and maybe she knew it too, and sooner or later they were going to have it out. But he kept putting off the inevitable—because he didn't want to distract her from her studies, because if he left her he'd have to find another flat or return to California, because leaving would mean having to make certain decisions he wasn't in the mood to make.

He didn't regret accompanying her to Verona when she'd won her grant to study Renaissance architecture. He'd hated the way his job was going, and he'd needed to put as many miles as possible between himself and his father. He and Rosalie had been a hot item back then. They'd had themselves a fantastic time.

But now that time was winding down. The fire had burned out; they were merely tiptoeing around the smoldering embers.

She had been out all morning, observing rehabilitation work on some ancient building. He'd spent the morning on the terrace, devouring the poetry of Gabriele D'Annunzio—high-flown distasteful stuff, but it was a good way to practice his Italian. Rosalie had returned to the flat for lunch, and afterward she'd settled at her desk and he'd headed for the door.

It had been like that for a month, now: he stayed in when she went out, and when she came in he went out. They were together only at mealtimes and late at night, in bed—although even there they weren't together much. There had to be something better. But he'd be damned if he knew what it was, let alone how to find it.

The courtyard was swarming with sightseers that afternoon. One group spoke German. Another group seemed to be Scandinavian, although he couldn't distinguish which Scandinavian nation they were from. A chatty crowd of British visitors posed for photos and quoted random lines of Shakespeare.

And the two women. One was high-fashion beautiful, with blunt-cut black hair, an angular face and a model's tall, delicate build. The other looked sturdier, her honey-colored hair pulled back from her face and pinned haphazardly, her shoulders shaping a strong horizontal line beneath her linen T-shirt, her legs sleekly muscled below the knee-length hem of her denim skirt. Her complexion was golden, her eyes a soft mossy green.

He wondered why she intrigued him more than her prettier friend. He wondered why she didn't saunter up to the Juliet statue the way her friend did, clamp her hand around the bronze arm and wish for love. Maybe she was already in love. Or maybe she didn't buy into such mystical nonsense.

He certainly didn't.

Shortly after arriving in Verona, Rosalie had dragged him to this small piazza. "We have to touch the statue so we'll have a wonderful affair," she'd explained.

"I like things just fine the way they are."

"Touch it anyway," she'd said, racing ahead and slapping her palm on the statue's arm.

He had refused to touch it. It was an idiotic old wives' tale, he'd said at the time, and he'd never been a big fan of Shakespeare, anyway.

Since that afternoon last fall, he had strolled past the piazza countless times without entering. He didn't know what had lured him through the arched alley and into the courtyard that afternoon. The roses, perhaps.

She was gazing at the roses now, her sunglasses perched on the crown of her head so she could absorb the lush velvet color of the petals. Her raven-haired friend was halfway down the alley, but the green-eyed woman lingered, studying the statue with obvious misgivings. He noticed the loose drape of her shirt over her breasts. He noticed the way her teeth caught her full lower lip and worried it.

She inched closer to the statue, then glanced at her friend, who was standing near the arch, shouting something at her—in English. American English.

"What have you got to lose?"

The woman inhaled and touched the statue. He felt a shock deep inside him, something fierce and jolting, almost painful. She flinched and drew her hand back abruptly, as if the statue had singed her.

Her eyes met his. Through the lengthening shadows, through the overgrown vines and the throngs of tourists, he stared into the brightest, most beautiful eyes he had ever seen and discovered that he was unable to breathe, unable to move or think.

She broke away and darted down the alley toward the street.

He had to follow her. Had to catch her, talk to her, gaze into those mesmerizing eyes once more.

But first, he had to touch the statue. No choice in the matter: he simply had to touch it.

SHE SHOULD HAVE FOUND the dark, echoing corridors that marked the perimeter of the Arena soothing. The air was cool and still, the towering ceilings shaped into perfect parabolas, the ground covered in sand. According to a pamphlet she'd picked up at the entrance, Verona's Arena dated back to ancient Roman times. In the arched portals and underground passages she could imagine gladiators suiting up, clanking their swords and praying to their gods before they marched into the open heart of the amphitheater and offered up their lives for the entertainment of Verona's citizenry.

She climbed the steep stone stairs to the open-air theater. The late afternoon sun bathed the circular rows of seats. She thought about football stadiums, about

Roman circuses...about the man in Juliet's courtyard.

She hadn't even noticed him until she'd placed her
hand against the smooth bronze of the statue. The moment she had, she'd felt as if some power had entered
her, forcing her gaze to him.

He had been lurking in the shadows of the wall-
climbing vines, a tall, virile man with thick, dark hair
tumbling in defiant waves around his face. His jaw was
shaded by a day's growth of beard, and his eyes were as
hard and black as onyx. The top few buttons of his shirt
were undone, offering a tantalizing glimpse of his sun-
tanned chest. His long legs were encased in snug-fitting
jeans. His sleeves were rolled to the elbow, revealing
sinewy forearms lightly dusted with hair. His only jewelry was a wristwatch on a wide leather band.

How she had managed to take in so much about him
was beyond her. All she knew was that his eyes had held
hers captive and his thin lips had parted in astonish-
ment, as if he'd been under the same strange spell as she
was.

She'd been right to be frightened. And she was sensible enough to bolt.

She'd found the Arena, paid her fee and hurried inside, hoping the curving catacomblike hallways would
calm her jittery nerves. Whoever the strange man by
Juliet's statue was, she would never see him again.
Whatever uneasiness she'd felt when she'd touched the
statue, she would recover quickly enough.

She climbed all the way to the top row of seats, which
rose at least five stories above the sandy floor. The sun
felt hot on her cheeks; the air smelled clean and fresh.

"Rubbish," she said aloud, enjoying the familiar
sound of her voice. She'd let Nancy's fanciful mythol-

ogy run away with her. So she'd touched a statue and spotted a good-looking man. Italy, she and Nancy had noticed, was full of good-looking men.

She wandered along the white marble bleachers, gazing up at the cloudless sky and down at the area of the theater where a stage set was undergoing construction. The fellow who'd collected her entry fee said that the amphitheater was currently in use as a summer opera house. The steel scaffolding that held banks of stage lights seemed absurdly out of place in the ancient stadium, yet she liked them. She liked the sense of continuity, of connection between the present and the past. Hundreds of years ago, people watched shows in this theater, and people today watched shows in the very same theater. Hundreds of years ago, Romeo and Juliet had fallen in love, and in the very same city today, people still fell in love.

Not because of the statue, she hastened to remind herself. Not because of some corny legend, or some lyrical tragedy about a pair of hotheaded teenagers who eloped against their families' wishes, but because people were people, and sometimes, when a woman gazed into a man's eyes, her heart told her things she might choose to listen to—if she was foolish, or brave, or both.

Climbing down the tiers of seats was almost as exhausting as climbing up them. She felt her thigh muscles tighten and stretch as she made her way carefully down from the top. She had to pick a path around a coil of electrical cables, step over some discarded lumber, avoid a stack of paint cans. Eventually she reached the exit into the enclosed corridor that ran the perimeter of the theater.

Moving from the glare of the sunlit arena to the cool shadows of the hallway left her momentarily blind. She halted, blinking in the darkness, filling her lungs with the musty interior air. Gradually she made out the shape of the looming overhead arches, a heavy wooden door leading to an underground passage, the unlit electric sconce protruding from one of the outer stone walls. She started toward the main entrance.

A hand reached out from a shadow and brushed her arm. "Don't run away."

It was less than a whisper, but she knew the voice belonged to a man. Glancing down at the hand on her arm, she recognized the gold watch, the leather wrist strap.

She didn't have to see his watch to know, though. Awareness spun the length of her body, similar to the wrenching tremor that had seized her when she'd touched the statue of Juliet and seen him.

Be logical, a voice rattled inside her brain. Otherworldly forces and magical statues didn't exist. This man, whoever he was, had stalked her. He had followed her to the Arena and hidden in the shadows until he could grab her. And now he had her.

"Oh, God." She didn't know whether she spoke the words aloud or just thought them, lived them, prayed them in her soul.

He was going to kill her. She was going to die in the gloomy circle of hallways under the ghost-filled amphitheater. He would murder her and drag her body to one of the dark underground passages and no one would find her for days. Nancy would spend a fortune keeping their room at the Leon D'Oro while she waited for the *polizia* to locate Gillian. Her father would get a telegram from the U.S. embassy: *"We regret to inform you..."*

"It's all right," he murmured, moving out of the shadows so she could see him better. Once again she took in his thick, windswept hair, his strong features, his sensuous lips, harsh nose and stubble of beard, and then his eyes, profoundly dark, infinitely dark.

She wanted to find reassurance in them, comfort, safety. But she saw an anguish that matched hers, and passion. Burning passion.

He bowed toward her, but she swiftly turned her head away. "Don't," she pleaded in a tiny, frantic voice.

"You touched the statue," he said. "So did I."

"So what?"

His hand skimmed up her arm to her shoulder, lightly, gently. "I can't help it."

It dawned on her, belatedly, that he was speaking American English.

His caress reached the sensitive skin below her ear, his fingertips exploring the feathery wisps of hair at the nape of her neck. "Take your hand off me," she whispered.

An endless minute passed before he did. In the absence of his caress, her neck felt chilly. "You touched the statue," he repeated.

"I don't believe in that garbage." She sounded appallingly tentative.

"Neither did I, until the instant you touched it." He seemed to fight some internal battle—and lose. Reaching for her again, he curved both his hands over her shoulders and dug his fingers into the muscles of her back, urging her an inch closer to himself, two inches closer.

She felt his warmth through her shirt, through her flesh. She felt his need as if it were her own.

"Kiss me," he said, angling his head to hers once more.

No, she thought, *no!* But her lips brushed his, sought his, softened against his as he covered her mouth with his own. She would have resisted, but she couldn't. It was as if someone else had taken over her body—and definitely her mind.

"I don't even know you," she protested, her lips rubbing his as she shaped each word.

He sighed and closed his arms around her. "It doesn't matter."

"Yes it does. Of course it does."

"If I told you my name, you still wouldn't know me."

"I can't kiss you if I don't know you," she argued, an utterly irrational attempt at rationality.

"You already have kissed me," he said, then moved his mouth over hers again. He slid his arms around her, urging her against him as his lips coaxed and teased. She felt liquid in his arms, hot and fluid against the lean, firm contours of his chest, his hips.

This was madness. She had to stop. She was Gillian Chappell, a hardworking student, an up-by-her-boot-straps success story, a newly minted lawyer. She was five thousand miles from home, in a land where she didn't know the language, in a building where a millenium ago, ancient Romans used to amuse themselves by watching mortals go at each other with swords. She was trapped in the arms of someone she didn't know, trapped by her own unreasonable hunger for him.

Just a kiss, she promised herself. A kiss wouldn't kill her; it wouldn't ruin her life. She could explain this as a momentary lapse, a brief bout of insanity. And then she could escape and pretend it had never happened.

Except that no kiss had ever affected her this way before. No kiss had ever sent her heart soaring, her pulse sprinting, her breasts burning with the need to be touched, her thighs aching with the need to be stroked, parted, opened to this stranger, this man. This was not a kiss she could forget.

"Please," she moaned, thinking she was going to demand that he let her go. But that was the only word she could speak. "Please..."

He lifted one hand to the back of her head, weaving his fingers into the disheveled locks and holding her steady as his tongue coaxed her lips apart.

A kiss won't kill you, she swore to herself, then sighed and met his tongue with hers.

She heard his groan, a sound as dark and shadowed as the air around them. He turned, pressing her to the wall and arching against her as his tongue thrust deep. She reached up, unsure of whether she was going to push him away or pull him closer.

She molded her hands to his bristly cheeks, traced the rigid line of his jaw with her fingertips, then skimmed them down to his neck. His skin was smooth and hot. Her hands came to rest at his open collar and he reached up and covered them with his own, clasping them in a way that seemed vaguely consoling, almost friendly.

His breathing grew deeper, huskier, as his tongue danced with hers, as his chest moved against her breasts. He drew her hands down to his waist and then released them, sliding his own hands up until he cupped the underside of her breasts.

"No," she breathed. The sensations flooding her were far too dangerous. A moment's madness was one thing—but this had to stop.

"I want you." His voice rasped along her nerve endings. "I want you."

"No."

He let his hands drop, and she reluctantly removed hers from his waist. She leaned back against the cool stone wall, gasping for breath, her eyes closed so she wouldn't have to look at him.

A minute passed, and he sketched his calloused finger along one of her cheekbones and then the other, luring her eyes open. His mouth curved in a wistful smile, but his gaze was deadly serious. "What are we going to do?"

"I don't know about you," she said, her voice unnaturally low and thick, "but I'm going to walk out of here and forget I ever met you."

"I don't think that's possible."

She closed her eyes again, sliding her palms over the uneven stones behind her, searching vainly for an anchor on which to steady her whirling emotions.

"I want to take you back to my flat," he said, "but I can't." He grazed her forehead with his lips as he spoke. "Where are you staying?"

"The Leon—no!" What was it about this man that he could sneak past her defenses so easily? Yes, he was gorgeous, but many men were gorgeous, and Gillian had never let herself be suckered by them. She wasn't about to tell this man the name of her hotel.

"We belong together," he said, his voice so low, so insinuatingly soft she could practically feel her self-protective facade crumbling like the ancient ruins of Verona. "Our bodies belong together. I want your legs tangled with mine and your hair spilling through my hands and—''

"Stop!" She clamped her hands over her ears. "This is ridiculous. You may sound like an American, but you've bought into the Latin-lover routine way too much. If you're a gigolo, mister, you'd better find another lady to bother.''

"I'm not a gigolo.''

"What are you?''

His gaze relented, his smile growing almost benign as he tucked an errant strand of her hair behind her ear. "I'm a visitor from America, like you.''

"What's your name?''

"Owen.''

Owen. It didn't sound like the name of a gigolo. It didn't sound much like anything. But his name humanized him in a way. She was marginally less afraid of him now that she knew he was Owen.

"What's your name?'' he asked.

"None of your business. I've got to go. If I don't get back to the hotel my friend will start to worry.''

"I'll take you there.''

"That won't be necessary—''

"I'll summon a taxi for you.''

"I can summon my own taxi.''

A sigh escaped him. "I just . . . I don't want to lose you.''

"Consider me lost,'' she said, even though she didn't move.

He took a step back, and she pushed away from the wall. Her legs nearly buckled, but she kept her balance and hoped he didn't notice how fragile and disoriented she felt. She was going to walk out of the Arena with her head high and her hands curled into fists. Once she

was back in the bright afternoon sunlight, her mind
would clear and she'd consign the entire incident to her
memory's circular file.

He fell into step beside her, his long, powerful strides
reminding her that she couldn't possibly outrun him.
Beyond the curve in the corridor she saw a slab of diffuse sunlight spilling in from the entry gate. She accelerated her pace and Owen accelerated his.

Out, she thought. *Just get outside and this will all be
over.*

They exited into the main piazza. It was filled with
pedestrians—stylishly dressed men and women taking
a stroll after work, young couples eating *gelati,* and
elderly men and women sitting on benches, watching the
activity around them through wise, smiling eyes. Gillian was safe here.

He searched the street for a cab, found one and waved
his hand. The driver coasted to a stop in front of them.

Owen opened the rear door for her, then leaned toward the driver's window. *"La conduca Hotel Leon
D'Oro,"* he said, handing the driver a five-thousand-lire
note.

She sank into the upholstery and shut her eyes once
more, letting the taxi sweep her away from her mysterious suitor. He was gone. It was over. The lunacy of
their wild kiss in the Arena was history. She would never
see him again.

With a sudden, terrified start, she sat upright. *La
conduca Hotel Leon D'Oro...* He had given the name
of her hotel to the driver. He knew where she was staying.

She groaned softly, alarmed by the thought that he
would follow her to the hotel, that he would show up
later that evening, that he would get there before this

taxi did and be sitting in the lobby when she walked through the elegant beveled-glass door. Or worse, that she would take the elevator up to the room and find Nancy gone and Owen there instead, waiting, believing that they belonged together.

She wasn't free of him yet.

And as fearful as she was, one small part of her was glad.

Chapter Two

He saw her everywhere. In the crowded plaza, by the city hall, in the splashes of water spewing from the fountain. He heard her voice in the cooing of the pigeons, in the laughter of the children scampering across the cobblestones, in the intimate murmurs of lovers sauntering past him, their hands enlaced and their heads bowed together. He felt her in the warm evening breeze. He tasted her on his lips.

This wasn't like him. He was twenty-eight years old, four years out of business school, a year away from the loathsome pressures of working at Moore Enterprises, being monitored and second-guessed and commanded by his father—and he viewed himself as a diehard cynic. He had grown up rich enough to know that wealth carried more weight than love, that poetry was for weaklings and power was its own reward.

So why was he wandering aimlessly through the piazza, seeing a tawny-haired, green-eyed woman in every shadow, every shaft of light?

He could go after her again; the hotel wasn't far from the piazza. Yet if she saw him she would flee. He knew she'd been afraid of him.

But she'd kissed him. In spite of her fear, she had taken his face in her hands and touched her mouth to his. And it had been like nothing he'd ever known before.

He had to see her again. *Had to.* The understanding possessed him, compelled him, directed his footsteps along Corso Porta Nuova, passing under the arch that marked the city's ancient wall. Over the hum of traffic, he heard the chug and sigh of a train pulling into the Verona station, and then the hiss of the Hotel Leon D'Oro's fountains spraying silver water into the sky.

What would he say to her? How could he convince her of something he wasn't sure he could even convince himself of? This whole thing was crazy. Why had he become instantly, incurably obsessed with her?

How the hell was he even going to find her when he didn't know her name?

He entered the hotel, ignoring its soaring ceilings and majestic decor. He'd been there before; he and Rosalie had dined in the hotel's restaurant on a few occasions. The prices were astronomical. His green-eyed woman must be rich. Not that that mattered. All that mattered was the woman. Having her. Taking her. Loving her.

A bemused laugh escaped him. He was obviously deranged—and in an odd way, he liked it. Just to let go for a fantasy-driven afternoon, just to cut loose, chase a whim, live an illusion, crave a woman so insatiably that logic fell by the wayside...

He actually liked it.

Strolling to the front desk, he asked where he might find a pay telephone. The concierge directed him down a short hall. He dialed the flat, told Rosalie he wouldn't be home for supper, and noted with some satisfaction that she didn't sound disappointed.

Then he returned to the hotel's sumptuous lobby, took a seat on one of the plush sofas and settled in to wait.

"WE CAN'T GO OUT for dinner," Gillian said, pacing frantically about the elegant room.

Nancy gazed lovingly at her new purchases, which were arrayed across her bed: the green suede boots, a black silk blouse, a necklace of hammered gold and earrings to match. "We have to go out for dinner," she argued happily. "I need an excuse to wear all this stuff."

"You can wear it in Venice tomorrow. Really, Nance—can't we just order room service tonight?"

For the first time since she'd waltzed into their hotel room laden with shopping bags, Nancy seemed aware of Gillian's edginess. "Are you all right?"

"Sure," Gillian said, sounding far from positive.

"You look a little pale."

"Visiting the Arena took a lot out of me." What an understatement, she thought wryly. Glancing toward the door, she noticed that Nancy hadn't fastened the safety bolt. "I really would prefer to stay in tonight," she said as she crossed the room and twisted the lock.

As if a dead bolt could keep Owen out.

Even though he wasn't in the room, she felt his presence permeating the atmosphere. She felt the fiery strokes of his tongue in her mouth, the virile strength of his hips pressing into hers, the intimacy of his hands combing through her hair, skimming her arms, nearing her breasts.

Every time she closed her eyes he overtook her, dark, menacing, alluring. Every time she drew a breath she felt him inhabiting her, filling her in a way that transcended mere sex.

I want you, he had said. *What are we going to do?*

She knew what she wanted to do—run for her life. Fly back to New Jersey. Hide under her bed.

Make love with her stranger. Owen. Her man.

"I just don't feel like myself tonight," she said, wondering if Nancy could hear the quiver in her voice.

"What you need is a good meal. The concierge made a seven-thirty reservation for us at *12 Apostoli.* He said it's a wonderful restaurant, and if we order the evening's special they'll give us free souvenir plates. It's in this quiet little alley—"

"An alley?" Gillian echoed faintly. A quiet little alley was...well, right up Owen's alley. Even if he had no way of knowing her destination, she didn't doubt his ability to be there, lurking in the shadows, lying in ambush, preparing to pounce.

"It sounds divine," Nancy went on. "Let's get all dolled up for our last night in Verona. Don't forget—we touched Juliet's statue. Maybe we'll meet our true loves tonight."

I've already met mine, Gillian almost blurted out. Feeling her cheeks grow feverish, she spun away from Nancy and stared out the window. Owen was *not* her true love. He was a slick operator, an American Don Juan looking for easy action. That she had let him kiss her was embarrassing. That she'd responded as strongly as she had was even more embarrassing.

"Are you sure you're all right?" Nancy asked.

Gillian leaned forward until her forehead touched the window's cool glass. Six floors below, cars sped along Viale Piave—Mercedes and Porsches, Ferraris and Alfa Romeos, vehicles that bore little relation to the six-year-old Ford she had bought from her father when he'd splurged on a new pickup truck last year. She stared at the speeding roadsters, wishing she could talk Nancy into staying inside their hotel room until it was time to catch the train to Venice tomorrow.

"Are you having stomach problems? You've been careful to drink only bottled water, haven't you?"

Good idea—she could lie and say she was suffering from nausea.

Damn. She ought to be able to tell Nancy the truth. They'd known each other since their first day at NYU law school. They'd spent their second and third years sharing an apartment on West Twelfth Street. They'd critiqued each other's taste in men, analyzed their opinions of love and marriage and consoled each other with Southern Comfort and ice cream over their discovery that the best-looking guys in Greenwich village were gay. They told each other everything.

But she couldn't bring herself to tell Nancy about Owen. The incident in the Arena was unforgivable. Kissing a strange man in a strange place, kissing him with such consuming desire she'd been able to put out of her mind the peril of what she was doing...

More than embarrassed, Gillian was ashamed of that insane interlude in the shadows beneath the amphitheater. She was even more ashamed that hours after she'd fled from him, thinking of his deep, devouring kisses in the passageway still aroused her.

"All right," she said, because she knew Nancy would continue to interrogate her if she insisted on staying in the room for dinner. "You can have the shower first, but don't take long. If we're going out to this divine restaurant in the alley, I've got to wash my hair." *So it will be beautiful in case I see him again,* she thought— then chastised herself for letting such an absurd notion enter her mind.

She didn't want to see him again. She didn't. She didn't.

She wondered how many times she would have to tell herself that before she began to believe it.

THE RESTAURANT WAS, indeed, divine. There was too much food—antipasto, pasta, main course, *formaggio* and *dolce*—and too much wine, and all of it was wonderful. Nancy had been right; what Gillian had needed was a good meal to restore her equilibrium.

She handed the maître d' her credit card, and then she and Nancy retired to the ladies' room. In the mirror above the sink she admired her reflection. Her afternoon adventure might have left her temporarily pale, but now she looked flush with health. Instead of berating herself, she ought to congratulate herself on having taken a walk on the wild side and survived. For nearly her entire life she'd been well behaved, her passion reserved for principles and scholarship. She had always dated the sort of men she could bring home to daddy. She hadn't exactly been a stick-in-the-mud, but the balance sheet of her soul had a whole lot more pluses than minuses on it.

But that afternoon, miles from home, she'd been reckless. She'd done something impetuous, rash, deliciously dangerous. And so what? After twenty-four years of virtuous living, why not?

Gillian was no longer feeling jeopardized. The episode in the Arena was fading from her memory. Owen was gone, a figment of her past. Someday—perhaps once she and Nancy had made it to Venice—she would tell Nancy what happened and they would laugh about it.

She and Nancy returned to the table, where her receipt and two painted souvenir plates awaited them. Amid a chorus of *"Buona notte's"* and *"Ciao's"* they made their way to the front of the dining room and out into the alley.

Street lamps and moonlight illuminated the cobblestones; light spilled from a few upper-floor windows, the wooden shutters of which were thrown open to the balmy evening air. Gillian and Nancy strolled toward an open patio nestled among the buildings, from which another alley led to the street.

"Gillian."

His voice emerged from the shadows, low and insinuating and painfully familiar. She felt the color drain from her face, the strength from her legs. Not only had he found her again, but he'd learned her name.

Unaware that Gillian had frozen in place, Nancy continued down the alley to the patio. Gillian opened her mouth to call to her, but before she could get her voice to function, he had stepped out from a recessed doorway and slid his hand over the nape of her neck, twining his fingers into her hair and dropping a light kiss on her temple.

She shivered. Her abdomen clenched. If she'd felt sophisticated a few minutes ago, now she felt petrified.

"Let me come back to the hotel with you," he whispered.

"I can't," she whispered back. "I'm sharing the room with my friend." As if that were the only reason to say no.

"We'll take another room."

"Please leave me alone." She knew she sounded feeble, yet she couldn't seem to force energy into her voice, not when his thumb was stroking seductively along the crease behind her ear, when his breath caressed her hair, when she felt the potent male heat of him invading every cell of her body. "How did you find out my name?"

"I saw your credit card at the restaurant. Gillian Chappell."

"You were in the restaurant?"

"Only long enough to learn your name."

"I'm going to have it legally changed as soon as I get home," she warned. "And I'm going to cancel my charge account, so—"

His soft, rumbling laughter silenced her—and then his kiss silenced her even more effectively. She wanted to search for Nancy, but her eyes lost focus as his tongue reclaimed her mouth and his arms closed around her. Her eyelids grew heavy, her blood grew hot and she seemed capable of nothing except sinking into his embrace and kissing him back.

She wasn't sure how long she remained kissing him, her heart beating against his, her body pressed to his. It might have been seconds, or hours, or an eternity. She ought to have felt imperiled, yet the tight circle of his arms gave her a curious sense of security, and the subtle movement of his hips against hers was beguiling. If only she were just a little more daring, a little more reckless . . .

Through a fog of sensation, she heard Nancy's voice. "Gillian? Are you coming?"

"In a minute," she managed.

"That close?" Owen murmured. "Me, too." He slid his hands down to her hips and rocked against her, stoking the fire inside her until she understood what he meant.

"Don't." She hid her face against his shoulder and wedged her hands between their chests, putting some space between his body and hers. Her breath was shallow and ragged. Her flesh tingled, burned, seethed with unfulfilled longing and a painful awareness of how well Owen could fulfill that longing if she let him.

She heard footsteps on the cobblestones behind her. "Gillian?"

She nudged Owen back into the alcove and cleared her throat. "There was a mistake on the bill, Nance. I'll be right with you. Why don't you go on ahead and see if you can get us a taxi?"

"Okay."

She watched Nancy head back down to the patio, around the corner and out of sight. Then she gave herself a mental kick. Why had she told Nancy to leave? Why hadn't she escaped from Owen when she'd had the chance?

What are we going to do? His question from that afternoon haunted her, demanding an answer. If only she could accompany him somewhere public and well lit, order a cup of espresso and have it out with him, find out precisely who he was and what he wanted.... But she couldn't imagine going anywhere with him without their crazed yearning for each other overwhelming them, making conversation impossible. Unnecessary. Undesirable, even.

His fingers continued to wander through her hair, his body to shelter her. "Tell me what you want," he whispered.

I want to be an idiot, to cast off all my sensibility and make love with you. "I want you to leave me alone."

"Why?"

"I don't know you. I don't trust you. I'm leaving tomorrow and I'll never see you again."

"Mia cara." His voice was even softer, his lips moving as light as air over her brow. "You could leave this instant, and we would still be together."

"Why me?" She felt as if she were pleading for her life. "Why did you choose me? My friend is prettier, and—"

"You touched the statue."

"So did Nancy. So do hundreds of women every day, I'll bet. Thousands every week."

"I don't want thousands of women every week. I want you. You can ask why again and again, Gillian. It doesn't matter. I want you."

His quiet certainty unsettled her more than all her earlier fears that he was going to attack her. She and Owen were caught up in something that had no reason, no solution. "You'd better let me go," she murmured, knowing in her soul that even if he did, she would never be able to outrun her need for him or his for her. She could take the train to Venice tomorrow, and fly back to the United States next week, and spend the summer learning her new job by day and cramming for the New Jersey state bar exam by night—and, as he'd said, it wouldn't matter. He would still want her. She would still want him.

Yet staying with him, descending into the shadows of a warm Verona night, into the unknown, into this stranger's magical arms...

She was too smart to do that. Too cowardly. Too sane.

"Goodbye, Owen," she said, appalled by the sudden blurring of her vision as her eyes filled with tears.

He tightened his arms around her for a moment, then released her and took a reluctant step back. *"Arrivederci,* Gillian." He brushed his fingertips over her lips, then turned and vanished down the alley and into the night.

She knew what *arrivederci* meant. Not goodbye, but till we meet again.

They would meet again. Somehow, somewhere, no matter how much she wished otherwise, they would meet again.

BESIDE HIM, Rosalie slept.

He lay awake, staring up into the dark, hearing the occasional honk of a horn in the distance, the occasional slam of a door along the narrow, twisting street below. A faint breeze ruffled the curtains, barely strong enough to enter the room and dance across his naked chest.

He was restless. Itchy. Incredibly frustrated.

He'd arrived at the flat an hour ago to find Rosalie preparing for bed. Without preamble he'd announced, "I'll be moving out tomorrow."

She had turned and stared at him with her wide-set, remarkably dry eyes, and said, "I guess it's about time." No tears, no histrionics, no regrets. No hesitation, no inner conflict, no turbulent emotion like what he'd seen in Gillian's eyes, no fear or desire or despair. Nothing at all.

Had he once fancied himself in love with Rosalie? No. This had never been about love. It had been about a year abroad, an adventure, an excuse to get away from California and his manipulative father. It had been about having fun with a woman he liked and admired.

And now... it was about time.

He had no idea where he would go. His return ticket to Los Angeles was good until August 1; he could spend another couple of months in Verona if he wanted, or leave town and travel. Money was no problem, and he had a working knowledge of French to go along with his fluency in Italian.

He could follow Gillian.

If he did, she would hate him.

Why me? she had asked. A damned good question.

He was the sort of person who excelled at having an explanation for everything he did. Every investment he recommended, every suit he purchased, every dispute he engaged in with his father and every deal he engineered without his father's input—he always had a reason. He didn't buy a car without first studying every available trade journal and consumer write-up. He didn't buy a box of cereal without first skimming the list of ingredients.

So why Gillian Chappell? Why her?

Because she had touched the statue. Because he had. Because nothing else mattered but that.

THE TRAIN STATION WAS nearly deserted at six in the morning. Nancy dragged her wheeled suitcase across the platform, issuing a mumbled tirade about how at least a dozen trains traveled between Verona and Venice every day and there was no reason on God's green earth why she and Gillian had to be on the first one out.

Gillian searched in vain for a vendor. If only she could buy Nancy a cup of cappuccino, her friend might be a little less grouchy.

That Gillian wasn't equally drowsy was a miracle. She assumed she was running on adrenaline alone; she hadn't slept all night. By four o'clock, she'd been tossing a few final items into her suitcase, gathering Nancy's toiletries into a neat pile and squinting at the Eurail schedule, plotting a wee-hours departure from Verona.

She had to get out of town before she saw Owen again. If she saw him . . . she would never leave.

"You'll fall back to sleep once we're on the train," she reassured Nancy, staring anxiously down the track, trying to spot the train. "And when you wake up we'll be in Venice, and we'll have the whole day to explore. It'll be worth it, Nance."

"Nothing is worth getting out of bed this early," Nancy grumbled, punctuating her complaint with a loud yawn.

Gillian noticed a dot of light in the distance, a locomotive's cyclops-like headlight. It grew infinitesimally bigger as the train approached the station at a crawl, chugging slowly along the track. A metal-on-metal rumble vibrated the length of the rails, and then a hissing and chugging as the train drew closer, closer.

Escape, Gillian thought. Deliverance.

With a loud, steamy wheeze, the train rolled to a stop. A porter opened a door to the car nearest them and reached down to take Nancy's bags. Gillian shot a quick look over her shoulder. No sign of Owen.

She turned and passed her suitcase to the porter. The engines idled noisily; a bell clanged and a voice yammered in Italian over a loudspeaker. Gillian lifted her foot to the first step, then glanced behind her one final time.

There he was—sprinting across the parking lot as if his life depended on it. Her mind commanded her to board the train and hide, but her heart cried out, *Faster, Owen, faster!*

"You were in such a hurry to get here," Nancy hollered down to her. "Why don't you climb on, already?"

He had reached the stairway leading up to the platform. The porter, mistakenly thinking she was having difficulty navigating the steps, took her elbow and guided her up into the car. From there, Nancy grabbed her hand and dragged her down the corridor.

At the first window Gillian halted. Owen was halfway up the stairs to the platform.

"What's wrong with you?" Nancy scolded.

Gillian ignored her. Her fingers grew cramped clinging to the window frame, feeling for the releases. Owen leaped up onto the platform and began jogging along the train, scanning each window, searching for her.

The latches came undone and she shoved up the glass. "Here!" she shouted.

He saw her and broke into a run. His hair flew back from his face, wild and dark. His eyes were wilder, darker. The wind flattened his shirt against his chest as he raced to her window.

The train lurched, its engine engaging.

She tried to memorize his face, his physique, every detail about him. She should have stayed in Verona, should have forgotten Venice, New Jersey, her job, her father, her life. She should have forsaken everything for this man.

This man she knew nothing about, other than his first name.

"Owen."

The train lurched again, then inched forward. He reached up as she leaned out the window. His fingertips grazed her cheek.

The train moved again, in earnest, rolling down the track, accelerating out of the station. She continued to stare out the window, watching as Owen remained motionless on the platform, his gaze never leaving her. Her cheek was warm where he'd touched it.

Damn the statue. Damn the legend. This was just a dream. It was time to wake up.

The train pushed eastward, and Owen shrank until he was just a dot of blue jeans, white shirt, black hair and dark eyes. Just a tiny, indecipherable figure receding into the past, into a quiet, aching place in the hollowest part of her soul.

Arrivederci, she whispered.

No, not *arrivederci.*

Goodbye.

Chapter Three

"Trust me," said Juliet. "I know what I'm about."

"I trust you with all my heart," Romeo assured her, "but dear wife, why those two? They were but strangers drawn together by the aphrodisia of a passing breeze, and that breeze has not blown upon them in nigh two years. They knew nothing of each other then, and even less of each other now."

"And what did you know of me when first we met?"

Romeo hesitated; Juliet took satisfaction in his momentary defeat. "I knew you were beautiful," he finally answered. "I knew that from the moment I saw you my heart was no longer my own."

"And I knew no more of you. When love's mischievous dart pierces man and woman, nothing more need be known."

"This is not love's mischievous dart," Romeo argued. "It is your mischievous meddling."

Juliet indulged her husband his occasional quarrels. Like all men, he stood stalwart in his own wisdom and doubted the intelligence of a mere woman, heeding his own counsel to the exclusion of hers.

"*You always assume the worst, my lord,*" she chided him gently. "*Remember how you believed I was dead when I was but deeply asleep?*"

"*Deeply asleep? Without a pulse, without a heartbeat, and your skin as cold as the tomb in which you lay! That silly Friar Lawrence dosed you with a miserable potion to make you fall into the slumber of death.*"

"*But I wasn't dead,*" she reminded him. "'*Twas you that drank the lethal poison.*"

"*Let us not recount our mournful history,*" he overrode her, obviously aware that she had won another round. "*I wish only to point out to you that the couple you selected so long ago in Verona seem a dreadful match to this day.*"

"*They're a perfect match,*" she insisted.

"*A perfect match? When they haven't even glimpsed each other since their parting two years ago?*"

"*Firstly, think upon their names,*" Juliet argued. "*Gillian Chappell. It sounds rather like Juliet Capulet, you must agree.*"

"*And next you shall be telling me that Owen Moore sounds like Romeo Montague?*" His tone reverberated with sarcasm.

"*Moore,*" Juliet replied, "*is constructed of the same letters as Romeo, rearranged.*"

"*Ah! Of course! How could I not see it? And that they live on opposite ends of the American continent, she in the east and he in the west—surely there is a good reason for that, too.*"

"*They need conflict,*" Juliet contended. "*Without conflict, their love is denied its greatest test.*"

"*Is the width of a continent and the expanse of two years sufficient conflict for this great test?*"

"More than time and distance stands between them," Juliet said, although she dared not provide Romeo with specifics. He was clearly in one of his negative humors, eager to dispute every position she presented.

"When first you saw Gillian and Owen in the courtyard," Romeo reminisced, "you said you wanted naught but a happy ending."

"There can be no happy ending without a beginning," she said. "There can be no happy ending unless two strangers let love fill their souls and carry them as far as they can go."

"And how far shall your star-crossed lovers go this time?"

She sighed. For Gillian Chappell and Owen Moore she wanted the happiest of endings. Yet the risks were great, the outcome unknowable.

How far would they go? "As far as fate can carry them," she whispered.

"Fate and the hand of my beloved bride," Romeo murmured, no longer contentious. "Bring them together, Juliet. Give them their chance."

"SANDIFER CHEMICALS," Owen announced.

The three other people in his office—Moore Enterprises's attorney, the firm's chief strategic analyst, and his mother—gaped at him.

Ben Voltz, the analyst, spoke first. "Owen, we've all read the prospectus, and there's no question the company is a promising acquisition. But it's not the sort of thing Moore Enterprises involves itself in. First of all, it's a chemical manufacturing company—"

"Perfumes and scents. They blend a lot of the big-name colognes and after-shaves, the designer labels. We're not talking about toxic sludge, Ben."

"—And it's in New Jersey. We've always concentrated on the West Coast, Owen. Your father—"

"My father isn't here," Owen said quietly. He avoided eye contact with his mother. A year after his father's stroke, she still tended to get weepy when forced to acknowledge that the old man was no longer running the company.

"Still," Ben persevered, "your father would have passed on this one."

Owen drummed his fingers against the leather-trimmed blotter protecting the high-gloss veneer of his solid teak desk. When he'd taken over Moore Enterprises, he'd shunned his father's massive office, with its expensive artwork and its dark walnut decor, and returned to his own smaller office, an eclectically arranged room featuring mismatched furniture, an area rug patterned after Picasso, and the ripest view of Los Angeles's smog anywhere in the building.

With his father currently housebound, Owen had done his best to make peace with the domineering man. There was no sense in cultivating the old resentments and bitterness. Owen's father had spent thirty years trying to mold his son into a miniature version of himself, and Owen had spent thirty years resisting and rebelling. His father's infirmity had brought about a cease-fire. Owen and Franklin Moore were actually getting along, finding small areas of agreement, sharing insights and opinions.

But Owen refused to fill his father's shoes. He'd never liked his father's taste, in footwear or anything else.

"My father might have passed on Sandifer Chemicals," he conceded. "But I'm not my father. What do you think, Marc?"

Marc Utrecht, the attorney, shuffled the papers in his lap and shrugged. "The work force at Sandifer is unionized. They've got a very strong, tight-knit local. Busting it is going to take a real effort."

"Who says we need to bust the union?"

"Your father—"

"My father isn't here," Owen snapped, swiveling away from his advisers and staring out the window.

Franklin Moore was renowned for his habit of buying companies and dismantling them, pressuring employees, renegotiating contracts, extracting concessions and, all too often, forcing out the unions. He'd made a great deal of money along the way. When it came to pure capitalism, Owen's father was a master of the game.

Owen saw things differently. Sure, he could make a nifty profit by buying some company, stripping it of all but its cash cows and striking such fear into the work force that they would agree to anything—cuts in pay, increases in hours, reductions in benefits—just to hang on to their jobs. But such strategies didn't sit well with him. He was convinced he could make plenty of money for Moore Enterprises without destroying people's lives in the process.

"Owen," his mother addressed his back.

He continued to stare at the dismal brown horizon visible through the panes of glass.

"Owen, your father knew what he was doing when he built this company."

"I know what I'm doing, too."

"Where's the rationale? Why in heaven's name do you want to buy this perfume factory in New Jersey?"

He closed his eyes against the polluted vista and exhaled. He had no rationale, nothing he could explain to his mother, Ben and Marc—although the possibility that he was doing it in heaven's name made as much sense as any other.

He had gotten the idea last Saturday night at a party of Rosalie's. She and Owen had become good friends after they'd stopped attempting to be lovers. Now happily married to a fellow professor at UCLA, Rosalie was determined to find a suitable partner for Owen. "I want you to be as happy as I am," she often said.

Owen couldn't imagine ever being that happy. Content, yes. Even tempered, sure. But happy? Joyously, excruciatingly happy?

Not bloody likely.

He enjoyed having Moore Enterprises at his disposal; he enjoyed being able to reshape the company to reflect his own views and values, even though his every effort was met with opposition from the triumvirate now seated around him. He liked his newfound financial clout, and he liked the fact that he could visit his father and talk to him, not as father and son or as mentor and acolyte, but as friends, companions, people who could disagree without blowing up at each other.

He liked the small, eccentric house he'd purchased south of the city, in Venice. He wasn't sure why he'd gravitated to the quirky seaside community, with its resolutely zany residents and its picturesque canals. During his year in Italy, he'd never gone to the original Venice.

He almost had. One morning, watching a train pull out of the Verona station, he had very nearly stormed the ticket office and reserved a seat on the next train out.

But he hadn't. What would he have done there? Continued to stalk Gillian like a maniac, trying again and again to seduce her, when she obviously didn't want to be seduced?

Instead, he'd gone home to California, determined to regain his balance. Ignoring his father's invitation to resume his position at Moore Enterprises, he'd purchased the house in Venice and begun investing his own money in a couple of promising local businesses. He hadn't had to bust unions or dismantle companies to make a profit. He'd done quite nicely with his holdings in an expanding chain of sandwich shops and a swimsuit boutique.

And then his father had suffered his stroke, and Owen had taken the helm of the family business, where he spent far too much energy trying to convince his mother and the other holdovers from his father's reign that "the way it's always been done" wasn't necessarily the right way or the best way.

Happiness, though—that had somehow eluded him. He was busy, pleased with his achievements and challenged to achieve more. He took long runs on the beach at twilight; he spent his Saturdays in refreshing solitude and his Sundays visiting his father at the house in Bel Air. He accepted Rosalie's matchmaking efforts good-naturedly, but none of the women he'd met since he'd left Italy ignited a fire inside him. None of them could make him lose his grip on reality the way Gillian Chappell had.

The few unattached women at Rosalie's house last Saturday night hadn't even tempted him to relax his grip. He'd exchanged pleasantries with them, declined politely when one tried to interest him in her telephone number, and slipped into the kitchen, where a couple of men were engaged in a technical discussion. Owen had opened the refrigerator in search of a beer.

"Sandifer," one of the men had said.

"Sandifer?" his companion had repeated.

"Yes. Sandifer."

Sandifer. Like a message from the chill depths of the refrigerator. *Sandifer.*

The following morning, in the business section of the Sunday paper, he'd found a tiny article about a specialty chemical company looking for a buyer. Located in north-central New Jersey, the firm was named Sandifer Chemicals.

"I don't care what my father might have done," Owen said, rotating his chair back to face the triumvirate. "We're going after Sandifer. Start the process, Marc."

"But Owen—"

"Do it. I'm right on this, okay?"

"How do you know you're right?" his mother argued.

How did he know? His gut told him, his intuition. Some strange whisper in the wind, sweeping down from above the canopy of smog, told him.

"I just know. That's all. I just know."

GILLIAN'S FINGERS WERE slippery with butter when the phone rang. "Can you get that, Nance?" she asked.

Nancy had been slicing cucumbers for a salad. She set down her knife and reached across the counter to the wall phone. "Hello? Oh, hi. Hang on, I'll get her." She extended the receiver toward Gillian. "It's your dad."

Gillian gazed at her half-buttered loaf of garlic bread. On the stove a pot of water was close to a boil; a stack of uncooked linguine sat on a plate beside it. Her sauce was simmering. Cooking Italian was something she and Nancy did every time Nancy escaped Manhattan to visit Gillian, even though their Americanized Italian cooking resembled the exquisite cuisine of northern Italy about as much as liverwurst resembled *pâté de foie gras*.

With a sigh, Gillian wiped her hands on her apron and took the phone from her friend. "Yeah, Dad, what's up?"

"You free next Monday afternoon?"

She laughed. "Sure. All I have to do is go to work and earn a living. Why?"

"We need you over at the plant. It's bad news, sweetheart. Sandifer's been bought."

"I'd call that good news. The current owners want to retire. They would have closed the place down if they hadn't found a buyer to take it over."

"They found a buyer, all right. Moore Enterprises."

"Moore?" Gillian cursed quietly. "You're kidding."

"I wish I was. The guys are in a panic, Gillian. You know what that Moore outfit does."

Gillian knew too well. Over the past dozen years, Moore Enterprises had established an odious reputation for acquiring businesses and threatening the workers with unemployment if they didn't renegotiate their contracts. As a lawyer specializing in labor issues, Gillian knew enough about Moore Enterprises to understand that her father and his fellow employees at Sandifer Chemicals had a good reason to be worried.

"Moore is based out in California," she said. "I hate to think they're spreading their tentacles all the way to New Jersey."

"Seems they are. Notices announcing the purchase went up today," her father confirmed. "A letter of intent's been signed, and the sale's been approved by the Feds. Some jerk from Moore is supposed to come by next Monday to meet with union reps. Any chance you can be there?"

"I can try," she promised, mentally reviewing her schedule. "What time?"

"One o'clock."

"I'll see if I can shift things around. I'm taking depositions on a class-action suit all morning. If it runs late, maybe I can get someone to cover for me."

"Do what you can. The guys are counting on you," her father said before hanging up.

Gillian cursed again. She lowered the receiver and turned to find Nancy wedging a clove of garlic into the garlic press.

"Hurry up and finish buttering the bread," Nancy commanded, reading Gillian's grim expression. "You can burst into tears later."

"I'm not going to burst into tears," Gillian promised as she picked up her knife and continued smearing butter onto the slices. "I'm going to resort to extremely unladylike language."

"Sounds like fun. Family dissension is such a joy."

"I'm not angry with my father," said Gillian, attacking the bread with her butter knife. "Ever hear of Moore Enterprises?"

"Sure," Nancy confirmed, tucking a silky black strand of hair behind her ear. "It's a big holding company out in L.A."

"It's a parasite," Gillian raged. "They buy companies, suck the life blood out of them and then spit out the bones."

"Spare me the melodrama," Nancy protested. "You seem to forget I work on Wall Street. Half my clients are parasites."

"None of them can be as bad as Franklin Moore. That guy is the nemesis of unions. He's a blight on the American worker. He's—"

"Now, now, Gillian," Nancy cooed, tossing the linguine into the boiling water and giving it a stir. "Your roots are showing."

True enough. As the daughter and granddaughter of union loyalists, Gillian wasn't ashamed of waxing emotional about labor issues. Her mother's family had been West Virginia coal miners and militant activists in the United Mine Workers. Her father's family was, as they joked, "in oil," working in the refineries of central New Jersey. Even if Gillian had succeeded in earning herself a superlative education, she never forgot where she came from.

"You know what your problem is?" Nancy asked, leaning against the counter and waving a cooking spoon at her.

Gillian wrapped the garlic bread in foil and popped it into the oven. "No, Nance," she said with a smile. "But I'm sure you'll tell me."

"You need some great sex."

Gillian rolled her eyes and laughed. "That's your solution to everything."

"Not *everything*," Nancy corrected her. "It's not my solution to the greenhouse effect or world hunger. Still, it's a good way to let off steam."

"I don't want to let off steam. I want to be mad as hell about Franklin Moore and his sleazy business practices."

"Gillian." Nancy hoisted herself to sit on the counter and regarded Gillian from her superior height. "You don't have to fall in love, you know. Just have a little fun."

"I *do* have to fall in love," Gillian mumbled. "If I'm going to sleep with someone, I mean. I'm a little old-fashioned that way."

"You weren't old-fashioned when we lived together on West Twelfth Street."

Gillian laughed. "Sure. I talked about sexual liberation all the time in those days—because it was only talk. In case you've forgotten, law school took up twenty-three hours out of every day. We didn't have time for sex."

"All I'm saying is, why don't you let me fix you up with someone? There are all these foxy single guys working at the top Wall Street firms. It doesn't have to be till death do you part. Just a few dates, some good times, a way to work off your passion."

Letting out a weary breath, Gillian busied herself sweeping the bread crumbs into the trash. It wasn't as if she hadn't gone on dates in the past few years. She'd met men, socialized, given it her best shot.

But passion? No. She'd spent all she had on a stranger in Verona two years ago.

At times she wondered whether that was why she'd wound up buying her tiny ranch house in Verona, New Jersey. She could tell herself she'd chosen the town because it was clean and pretty and removed from big-city crime. But she couldn't deny that something more had been at work when she'd chosen this address, something subliminal.

A desire to feel that passion again, the passion she'd known only once before, in another town called Verona.

When was she ever going to get over him? Two years had passed, yet she still couldn't kiss a man without remembering what it had been like to kiss Owen, to feel his hunger illuminating her soul, to know that hunger and share it.

Great sex? There was only one man in the world she could think of in that context, and she'd run from him. She'd turned her back on everything he'd offered—which wasn't much, she reminded herself time after time. But she could have had that passion, could have experienced that ecstasy with Owen.

And she'd run away.

"How's the linguine?" she asked in an artificially bright tone. *"Al dente?"*

Nancy scooped a strand from the pot and tasted it. "More *al* than *dente.* Let's open that bottle of Soave, Gillian. If great sex is out of the question, we might as well get drunk."

"Might as well," Gillian agreed. If she didn't get drunk, she would probably spend the night fuming about Moore Enterprises and its nefarious plans for Sandifer Chemicals.

Either that, or she'd spend the night dreaming of Owen. Again.

She grabbed the bottle, uncorked it, and filled her glass to the rim.

HE SHOULDN'T HAVE BEEN surprised that everyone at Sandifer Chemicals treated him gingerly. Depending on their perspective, he was either a noble prince who had saved the company from shutting down or a dreaded agent of change, one who carried his father's reputation on his back.

Since Ben Voltz had started negotiations on the purchase agreement a month ago, Owen had had an opportunity to examine the company's books more closely. He saw no reason to disband the union local; his father would have done so on principle, but Owen figured that the company would be more apt to maintain its profitability if its work force remained undisturbed. However, fat could be trimmed. He had traveled to Morristown both to assure the folks at Sandifer and to assert himself.

"Anything you need, Mr. Moore, anything we can do to help you out, you just let us know," said the obsequious middle-aged man who had met him in the lobby of the nondescript white building that housed Sandifer Chemicals. He'd introduced himself as John Balthasar, Sandifer's comptroller, and he wouldn't shut up. "You can choose any office you'd like as your local base of operations, Mr. Moore. We'll just rearrange the staff to accommodate you. I mean that."

"I wasn't planning on settling in here," Owen said. "I don't know what I'd need an office for."

"Oh." Balthasar appeared uneasy. "Are you going to turn around and sell us again?"

"No. I'm going to leave you pretty much alone."

Balthasar's face brightened. "Leave us alone! That's just fine, Mr. Moore, just fine. Here, let me get that door for you...."

And on and on, fussing over Owen, treating him like royalty, presenting him with a flourish to secretaries, accountants and quality-control technicians, apologizing for the fact that the men's room looked like any other men's room in any other manufacturing plant.

Owen did his best to smile and act thrilled to meet all the people Balthasar kept thrusting at him, but the longer his tour of Sandifer Chemicals dragged on, the more he wished he could go back to his hotel room.

He couldn't, though. He had to meet with the union representative.

"Right this way, sir," Balthasar said, holding yet another door open for him. They entered a brightly lit room, walled in cinder block and furnished in Formica and vinyl. A set of vending machines hummed in one corner; a coffee machine burbled in another. "This is one of the employee lounges," Balthasar said, hustling over to an interoffice telephone on the counter that ran along the wall below the windows. "I'll just let the guys from the line know you're here."

"Good." Owen set his leather briefcase on a table, rolled his shoulders beneath the jacket of his summer-weight wool suit and tugged at the knot of his tie. The air conditioner didn't work well in the plant. The corridors were too drafty, the rooms too stuffy. He wondered how much an overhaul of the ventilation system would cost.

John Balthasar spoke into the phone for a moment, then hung up and beamed at Owen. "They're on their way. Can I get you some coffee?"

"No, thanks."

"Would you like to sit? I know these chairs aren't that comfortable, but..."

Owen eyed the molded plastic chairs and shrugged. "They'll do."

"Anything else you need?"

He sized up the eager man. "Tell me, Mr. Balthasar. These men I'm about to meet—how much do they hate me?"

"Hate you?" Balthasar erupted in a phony belly laugh. "What makes you think they hate you?"

"I'm their new boss."

"Oh, yes, well..." His smile faded. "I suppose they're a little apprehensive. Perfectly understandable under the circumstances."

"Yes."

"Matter of fact, sir, one of them invited his daughter to participate in this meeting. She's a labor lawyer up in Paterson. Nice girl, though. I'm sure she won't cause you any trouble."

A labor lawyer? It sounded as if the employees were girding for combat.

"Her father, on the other hand..." Balthasar leaned toward Owen conspiratorially. "He's a firebrand, know what I mean? Shop steward and an officer in the local. One of those 'solidarity forever' types. He's been talking to anyone who'll listen about what you might do to the place. I'd watch out for him if I were you."

"And his daughter?"

"Smart, but nice. She knows her manners. Her mother died a long time ago, but she's turned out well. She's a pretty popular girl around here."

Owen swallowed his distaste for John Balthasar. He didn't like men who gossiped disloyally about their colleagues, or men who referred to full-grown women as girls.

Behind him the door opened and three men trooped in. Owen immediately figured out which one was the leader. Not because he was older than the other two, not because he walked a step ahead of them, but because of his bearing, his aura of authority. Clad in pale denim coveralls, a pair of protective goggles dangling on an elastic strap around his neck and thick-soled work shoes on his feet, he stood nearly as tall as Owen, his silver hair slicked back from a weathered, handsome face, his chin strong and his eyes surprisingly green.

Owen experienced a twinge of recognition, but he quickly dismissed it. Lots of people had green eyes. He just happened to be extra sensitive when it came to that particular color.

The man and his two sidekicks strode briskly around the table to face Owen, as if they wanted a four-legged Formica barrier between him and themselves.

John Balthasar stepped forward. "Mr. Moore, I'd like you to meet Peter Hrubcek, one of our newest employees...." He gestured toward the youngest of the threesome, who gave Owen a nervous glance and a feeble handshake. "And this is Craig O'Hara...." He indicated the huskiest of the three, a robust fellow with a sunburned nose and a handshake as bruising as Hrubcek's was anemic.

"And last but certainly not least, Sam Chappell, the shop steward here at Sandifer Chemicals. Sam, this is Owen Moore."

Chappell.

No. It was impossible. Just a coincidence. Except for the man's eyes, Owen would never had made the connection.

He shook Sam Chappell's hand and met the man's flinty, confrontational stare. "It's a pleasure," he said.

"I can't say the same," Sam Chappell retorted, his eyes hard with anger. "I know what you stand for, Mr. Moore. I know what you do when you acquire a new business and I don't like it."

"Mr. Chappell—"

"You fly around the country in your fancy five-hundred-dollar suits, buying companies and coercing

hardworking men and women to bend to your will.
Well, let me warn you, Mr. Moore, we're not going to
knuckle under here. The men and women on the line at
Sandifer are united. We're not going to bend.''

Owen would grant the man a few points for candor.
He felt self-conscious about his custom-tailored suit,
which had cost significantly more than five hundred
dollars. ''Mr. Chappell,'' he said calmly. ''Let's not
draw swords yet. I came here to talk, not to coerce anyone.''

''That's not the way your holding company has done
it elsewhere. We know what you stand for, we know
your modus operandi. We aren't fools, Mr. Moore. We
didn't come to this meeting expecting to lie down and
die. We came prepared to fight. As a matter of fact,
we—''

Owen heard the door open behind him, but he didn't
dare to break from Sam Chappell's lethal stare. To turn
away would reveal weakness, and no matter how wrong
Chappell was about Owen's motives or his methods,
Owen had no intention of letting the man think he was
weak.

''Ah, here she is,'' Sam Chappell said.

''Sorry I'm late,'' came a voice behind Owen. A
woman's voice, lilting and slightly breathless and so familiar he flinched.

Inhaling for strength, he turned around.

She was standing in the doorway, her hair a tumble
of honey-colored waves, her white linen suit, turquoise
blouse and pale nylons dotted with raindrops, her face
devoid of cosmetics and her arms cradling a battered
leather portfolio. A gold watch banded her slender
wrist; unobtrusive gold hoops adorned her earlobes.
And her eyes . . .

Green. As green as the vines climbing the walls of a courtyard in Verona. As green as the ocean a block from his house in Venice. As green as a quiet glade in the most private reaches of his soul, a secret place no one had inhabited since a morning two years ago when a train had carried her away from him.

At last he knew why he'd had to buy Sandifer Chemicals, why he'd flown across the country, why he'd defied logic and the advice of his closest associates, and come to New Jersey.

For Gillian.

He'd come for Gillian.

Chapter Four

Owen.

How many times in the past two years had she dreamed of him appearing unexpectedly, returning to her, reaching out from the depths of a shadow and drawing her into his arms?

Too many times. And in each instance she'd called herself a fool.

Yet here he was, standing not in a shadow but in the glaring fluorescent light of the first-floor lounge at Sandifer Chemicals. A room where she used to sit and read Nancy Drew books on weekends when her father was assigned an extra shift and he didn't want her staying home alone. A room where she'd come one day after school, grabbed her father in a hug and shrieked, "I got into Rutgers! With a scholarship!" A room where she'd had her chin chucked and her pigtails tugged by her father's pals, where she'd practiced her multiplication tables, where she'd played marbles and hawked Girl Scout cookies and helped the lunchroom ladies string Christmas decorations in December.

Owen was in this room, and she would never be able to think about it in the same way again.

"This is my daughter, Mr. Moore," her father was saying. "She's an attorney, and she's here to make sure you don't try any fast moves."

Gillian almost blurted out that she was quite familiar with Owen's fast moves. But her father's words tripped off an alarm in her brain.

Mr. Moore?

"How do you do?" he said, his voice giving nothing away even as his dark, penetrating eyes spoke volumes. He extended his right hand to her. "I'm Owen Moore."

Mustering her courage, she slipped her right hand into his—and discovered that no amount of courage could have prepared her for the possessive warmth of his grip, the understated strength of his long, blunt fingers, fingers that had once woven deep into her hair and held her mouth to his. Her body responded all over, her breath growing short, her heart thundering against her rib cage.

"I'm Gillian Chappell," she said in a near whisper, her gaze locked with his.

A private smile flickered across his lips. "It's a pleasure."

No, she wanted to argue, *it's a danger. It's a catastrophe waiting to happen.*

She felt as if he'd held onto her hand forever, yet when he released it she realized it had been only a few seconds. She unconsciously flexed her fingers, trying to shake off the sensation of his touch.

"I promise you, Ms. Chappell," he said, being tactful and courteous, "I'm planning nothing that Sandifer's employees will need an attorney to protect them from."

"I'm here to make sure of that," she countered with admirable poise, clutching her briefcase in front of her and circling the table to her father's side.

Once she'd taken her chair, the men sat. The advantage of having a table between her and Owen was negated by the drawback of having to look straight at him. His cheeks were smooth, his complexion a warm, sundrenched tan, his hair impeccably trimmed. His suit had obviously been tailored to his lanky build. Around his left wrist he wore a watch on a thick leather band. Recognizing it, she fought off a treacherous shiver of memory.

Owen began to talk. He seemed oblivious to her as he pulled a folder out of his attaché case and slid it across the table to her father. "Moore Enterprises' purchase of Sandifer Chemicals marks a new direction for us," he said. "Not only have we never acquired a chemical company before, but we've never before done business the way I intend to do business with you."

Her father shuffled through the papers in the folder and frowned skeptically. Gillian knew she ought to study the papers with him, but she couldn't stop gazing at Owen, observing the glint of fire in his dark eyes, the graceful strength in his hands, the motions of his mouth as he continued to speak. Instead of paying attention to his words, she absorbed the smoky timbre of his voice, his inflections, his confidence.

Cara mia, he had once murmured to her. *Arrivederci.* Till we meet again.

"Now, here's a problem right off the top," her father said, breaking into Owen's monologue. "This change in the health insurance..." He glanced toward Gillian, and she sat up straighter and tried to focus on a paper bearing the title *Health Plan Options.* "You see, this is exactly what we're worried about, Mr. Moore. You people try to shove this stuff down our throats—''

"I'm not shoving anything down your throats, Mr. Chappell."

"In the past, we got the health-maintenance organization coverage for free. It was part of the union contract."

"Do you have any idea what health insurance costs?" Owen sounded much more composed than Gillian's father. "What we're offering is three different health plans. The least expensive one is available to Sandifer employees for free. If they choose one of the more expensive plans, all they have to pay is the difference."

"We're used to getting full coverage for free," her father grumbled, eyeing Gillian in search of support.

She perused the page and shrugged. "I hate to say it, Dad, but his proposal is in line with what a lot of companies are doing these days. It's better than many."

"It's not right," her father muttered.

And on they went, debating, bickering, her father exuding hostility and Owen exuding patience. If Gillian's presence troubled him, he gave no indication of it. He was all business.

She sized him up, not as a woman who'd once been insanely smitten with him, but as a professional familiar with the way Moore Enterprises operated. She had always heard that the Los Angeles-based outfit was ham-fisted in its negotiations—or, more accurately, that they didn't negotiate at all.

But Owen was playing his role as the new owner with great diplomacy.

Maybe it was an act. Maybe once the workers shook his hand and left the room, Owen was going to tear up all his lovely documents and raid the pension fund.

Maybe he was romancing her father and his fellow
workers with the same alluring magnetism with which
he'd romanced her two years ago. "These health policies don't matter," she could imagine him purring in
that low, irresistible voice of his. "You touched the
statue. I want you."

I want you.... Her thighs ached; her breathing became shallow. Discreetly she shifted in her chair and
smoothed her skirt over her lap.

"I don't trust you!"

Her father's booming voice brought her attention
back to the meeting. She looked up to see him jabbing
a finger at Owen. "I don't trust what he stands for," he
yelled at her. "I know what he's done to other companies, and I don't trust him."

"Let me earn your trust," Owen offered, his gaze still
on Gillian. She wondered if he was as transfixed by her
as she was by him, or if he simply saw her as the weak-
est of the four people facing him across the table.

She wasn't weak—at least not when it came to his
proposals. If there had been something to fight about
in his folder of policy changes, she would have fought
with everything she had. But she saw nothing to rebel
against. What Owen was proposing for the company
was neither revolutionary nor unjust.

When it came to Owen himself, however, to the un-
nerving darkness of his eyes, the heat of his gaze, the
long-suppressed memories trembling to life inside
her...yes, she felt weak. Helpless. As susceptible as
ever.

"Look," she said, deliberately glancing at her watch,
although what it said failed to register on her. "I've got
to get back to my office. Why don't you let me review
Mr. Moore's proposals on my own?" With a wary smile

at Owen, she added, "No one is going to commit to anything right now. We'll study what you've got here and let you know if we find anything unacceptable."

"You won't," he assured her. "I'm a very fair man."

She had to stifle a scornful laugh. He hadn't been fair in his dealings with her two years ago. She'd tried to reason with him—and he'd kissed her. She'd tried to cling to her sanity, and he'd gathered her in his arms and filled her mouth with his tongue and rocked his hips to hers, inviting her, luring her, stealing her ability to think.

"So, if you'll all excuse me," she said, rising to her feet, "I've got to run."

Don't run away.

She thought he'd actually spoken, then realized that her mind was playing tricks on her. She had heard his voice only in her mind, in her soul, echoing the first words he'd ever said to her: *Don't run away.*

She definitely had to run.

She was dimly aware of the other men standing, of her father kissing her cheek and murmuring something about seeing her at Lettie and Charlie's that evening. She heard Craig O'Hara remind her to use a high-acid fertilizer on her azaleas and John Balthasar making one of his stupid remarks about how she got prettier every time he saw her, and then she was out of the lounge.

Running.

She didn't slow down until she was in the parking lot. The cool drizzle roused her from her daze. She stood on the sidewalk outside Sandifer's drab white headquarters, sucking in lungfuls of damp May air, feeling the raindrops prick her cheeks and snag in the unruly waves of her hair.

It's all right, she whispered. *He's a Moore, one of the bad guys. You got away in time.*

Yet she felt no more triumphant now than she had that morning at the train station in Verona, watching Owen watching her, seeing him recede as the train carried her out of his life.

Now he was back in her life. And he was the Moore in Moore Enterprises, one of the most rapacious conglomerates to have ever plied the capitalist trade. He stood for everything she abhorred, every injustice that had ever been committed against workers.

Well, she wasn't powerless. She was a lawyer. And if his company dared to cross her father's union the wrong way, she'd see that he paid.

She headed across the lot to her car. The old heap refused to start.

The string of curses she released was more foul than was called for. Five times out of ten, her car wouldn't start in a light rain. She knew what to do, how to get it to work. This was no great tragedy.

But she wanted to get the hell away from Sandifer before...

She just had to get away.

She was leaning across the engine, carefully trying to keep her white jacket from brushing against anything grimy as she wiped the battery leads dry, when she heard him calling. "Gillian!"

More curses spilled out of her, curses she hadn't even known she knew. Yet there was no edge of anger in her voice. Only defeat, despair...dread.

"Gillian." He was getting closer, his footsteps swift and light against the asphalt. Staring at the engine, she saw not the battery but Owen jogging through the train station, his hair longer and less well groomed, his body clothed in jeans rather than an exquisitely styled suit—but there was no difference between that man and this one in his determination to reach her. There was no difference between her memory of him and the reality of him. In both incarnations he was tall, attractive, bold, resolute . . . overpowering.

Her hands fisted around the rag as she straightened up and turned to confront him. The light rain dampened her cheeks like tears.

He slowed to a stop in front of her. He was carrying a folder, which he tossed into her car. "Here's a copy of the documents I gave your father," he said. "You left so fast, I couldn't give them to you."

She glanced at the folder, at the rag she was convulsively wringing, then at his hands as they closed around hers. "I'm sorry," he said.

An apology? Was he going to destroy the union, after all?

Was he going to break her heart? She had absolutely no doubt that he could if he wanted to.

"Why are you sorry?" she asked warily.

"This was the wrong way for us to meet again."

She watched as the raindrops darkened his already black hair, streaked down his sun-burnished cheeks, glittered in his eyebrows and beaded on the fine fabric of his jacket. "Was there a right way for us to meet again?"

"I don't know." His thumbs stroked the backs of her hands, tracing the smooth skin, the narrow bones. "It doesn't matter."

"Nothing matters to you, does it?" she snapped, her emotions spilling over in a rage. "That's what you said to me then, and you're still saying it. It doesn't matter.

Well, let me tell you something, Mr. Moore—it *does* matter.''

A slow smile tugged at his lips. "What matters?"

Her shoulders sagged. "I don't know."

"Here's what matters," he said, still stroking the backs of her hands, sending ripples of heat up her arms. "We found each other. We're together."

"Coincidence," she argued, willing herself not to take pleasure in the shimmering sensations his thumbs imparted to her, willing herself not to wish he was alone with her somewhere private and dark, where he could touch more than just her hands. "You aren't here for me. You're here because your bloodsucking company likes to buy up other companies and squeeze every dollar you can out of them. And then, when there's nothing more to take, you like to walk away and leave the ruins for someone else to clean up. That's why you're here."

His hands fell still around hers. His eyes grew darker, harder; his smile faded. "That's a pretty harsh judgment."

"I'm a labor lawyer," she reminded him. "I know what Moore Enterprises does to other companies."

"I'm not my father. I do things differently."

"Why should I believe you?"

He stared at her a moment longer. Then, without warning, he hauled her against him. She felt the rag slip from her fingers, felt her strength ebb from her legs as he crushed his mouth to hers. The moment his tongue met hers in a conquering surge, she believed everything and nothing. Everything mattered—and nothing did.

Nothing but this. Him. Owen.

The dampness on her cheeks was too warm to be raindrops. She pulled her lips from his and hid her face against his shoulder. "Don't make me crazy again," she murmured, her lips brushing against the fine fabric of his suit. "I like being sane."

"I want you," he said, as if she hadn't spoken. "Even more now than two years ago."

"You still don't know me," she argued, wondering why logic seemed as irrelevant now as it did then.

"I know you're a lawyer." He drew back and studied her rain-wrinkled suit and subdued jewelry. "Were you a lawyer then?"

"I had just finished law school," she answered. It seemed a trivial thing to be discussing, especially after the shattering intimacy of his kiss. But given how little they knew of each other, she figured they had to start somewhere. "Were you a corporate shark then?"

A quiet laugh escaped him. "No. I was a rich kid looking for fun."

Well. That was blunt. "And now you've decided that taking over my father's factory and destroying his union is fun."

"You were in there, lady lawyer. Did you see me destroy his union?"

"No, but—"

"I have no interest in destroying your father's union, or your father, or Sandifer Chemicals. I bought the company. I want to see it prosper. I want my employees happy. That's all there is to it."

That wasn't all there was to it, and Gillian knew it. She just didn't know what more there was. "Why Sandifer?" she pressed him. "Why?"

A wry grin twisted his lips. "Do you really want to know?" At her solemn nod, he confessed, "I heard voices."

"Voices?"

"My head was inside a refrigerator at the time."

In spite of herself, she laughed. "Oh, God. You're even crazier than I am."

His smile was gentle, almost sweet. "Really, Gillian—it doesn't matter why I heard voices, or where I heard them. Sandifer Chemicals brought us together. I didn't know it would, but it did. Isn't that enough?"

She supposed it was, when one was rich and looking for fun. She couldn't imagine herself going out and buying a chemical company because she heard voices in a refrigerator. "Look, Owen, I have to get back to my office."

She bent over to retrieve the fallen rag. He was quicker, plucking it from the ground and handing it to her. "What's wrong with your car?"

"When the battery gets damp it acts funny." She busied herself drying the leads, grateful for the excuse to turn her back on him.

"Are you free this evening?"

"No."

She felt him behind her, felt the shadow of his hand an instant before it alighted on her shoulder and eased her around. "Are you seeing someone else?" he asked.

It was none of his business, but she answered anyway. "No."

He smiled enigmatically. "Have you seen anyone else in the past two years?"

"Of course I have. Lots of people. Hundreds."

His smile expanded into a soft chuckle. "Neither have I," he admitted.

She couldn't maintain her lie in the face of his honesty. "You haven't?"

"I've tried. A dinner here, a movie there. But... There's been nobody. Nobody but you."

There wasn't me, she wanted to shout. Except that that, too, would be a lie. The dates she'd gone on since Verona had failed to erase Owen from her thoughts, from her heart. The men she'd met had been nice, pleasant companions, but she'd felt nothing in their arms, nothing in their kisses to burn away her memory of Owen's passion.

His eyes, profoundly dark but luminous with desire, with resolve, held that passion now. She recalled her fear the first time she'd seen him—and even before she'd seen him, when she'd touched the statue and understood that she had somehow relinquished control over her own destiny.

She was still afraid. "What are we going to do?" she asked, wondering if he could hear the edge of panic in her voice.

"See me tonight."

"No. I really can't."

"Why not?"

"My aunt and uncle are having a barbecue."

"A barbecue?" He glanced up at the leaky rain clouds. "Not in this weather."

"A little drizzle never stopped Aunt Lettie from anything." She silenced herself. She was under no obligation to explain her aunt to Owen.

"A barbecue," he repeated, brushing a raindrop from his forehead. "Why don't you bring me with you?"

"Are you kidding? My father would throw you on the grill and baste you."

"He's going to be there?"

"It's a family get-together. We're watching the basketball play-off game."

"Let me come. Maybe in less adversarial surroundings I could communicate better with him."

"Any place where you and he are together is going to be adversarial. No, Owen. You can't come."

Another raindrop hit his forehead, but he ignored it. Gillian watched it skitter along the edge of his eyebrow and down his temple. "Where do your aunt and uncle live?"

"I mean it, Owen. You can't come."

He sighed. "Can I see you tomorrow?"

His persistence rattled her—but she couldn't help taking it as a compliment. "I don't know."

"When you do know, tell me." He curved his hands around her upper arms and pulled her gently toward him. His mouth brushed over hers, soft, seductive. "I'll be here all afternoon, probably till around five or so. Call."

"I don't think I'll have time. I've got tons of work to do. I'm putting together a class-action sex-discrimination case, and we've been interviewing parties to the complaint, and . . ."

"Call. Call and tell me when I can see you."

"Please don't push me, Owen. This whole thing is so strange. . . ."

He touched his lips to hers once more, then released her and backed away. "Don't fight fate, Gillian. Call me. I'll be here."

Here. He had always been *here,* she realized. Ever since she'd touched that damned statue he'd been *here,* a part of her, haunting her.

"I won't call," she said, slamming down the hood and flinging the damp rag on top of the folder he'd left on the passenger seat. Then she got in behind the wheel. "Finish your business and go back to California."

He gave her a seductive smile. "I'll see you. If not tonight, tomorrow. Or the next day. That's a promise, Gillian—I'll see you again. Soon."

She tried to yank her door shut, but he was holding it. He closed it for her, slowly, chivalrously. His smile was much too confident.

She hated him, hated herself, hated whatever ludicrous voices had brought him to New Jersey, whatever brainless impulse was making it so hard for her to drive away. She hated Moore Enterprises and Sandifer Chemicals, his father's vicious business practices and her father's out-of-date views. She hated everything, everything in the world that was conspiring against her, thwarting her, sapping her of will.

And most of all, she hated the truth. But she was too wise to reject it.

She was going to see him again.

Chapter Five

At four o'clock he was still in the lounge, wrangling over the new overtime calculations with Gillian's father. The other two workers had returned to the manufacturing wing and John Balthasar had returned to his office, leaving Owen and Sam to wage their battle one-on-one.

Sam Chappell had a chip on his shoulder the size of a sequoia. Everything Owen proposed Sam objected to. Every explanation Owen offered Sam rebutted or dismissed. Nothing Owen could say or do seemed to make any difference; Sam Chappell was determined to oppose him.

Ordinarily, Owen wouldn't have cared. He was used to rancorous business dealings. He'd fought plenty of skirmishes in his professional life—and though he'd won most, he had suffered a few defeats. It came with the territory.

But this was different. This was Gillian's father.

Owen wondered whether Sam had sensed Owen's desire for Gillian. He wondered whether Sam had detected the undercurrent passing back and forth across the table between Owen and Gillian, the invisible cords of passion pulling at them, binding them. For all Owen knew, Sam's antagonism might have nothing to do with Moore Enterprises' reputation as a corporate piranha. It might simply be that he'd seen the blatant yearning in Owen's eyes, and he'd seen that yearning mirrored in his own daughter's eyes.

How could Sam know about him and Gillian, though? What could he possibly suspect? Nothing had occurred between them, other than a few kisses.

And if she didn't call, nothing more might occur.

He tried to concentrate on the proposals, on the openly hostile man facing him across the table. But Owen was too conscious of the silent telephone on the counter by the window, too conscious of the hours ticking away.

She had to call. She had to. If she didn't...

He refused to contemplate the prospect of never seeing her again, never taking her in his arms and letting her know the full force of his love. For two years he'd been waiting—he hadn't understood precisely what he was waiting for, but he'd recognized that there was something lacking in his life. And now, at long last, what he needed was within his reach.

But only if Gillian called him.

Four-fifteen. Sam Chappell was fuming and sputtering over Owen's recommended method of computing raises.

Ring, he implored the phone. *Ring, damn it.*

Four-thirty. Sam objected to the layoff warning period. "Two weeks isn't sufficient. It's got to be four weeks, minimum. My people won't stand for anything less."

Owen jiggled his pen. He raked his hair back from his face. He talked about the need for flexibility and made promises about the speedy rehiring of laid-off workers. He loosened his tie.

Why hadn't she called? What the hell was she waiting for? Wasn't her longing for him as desperate as his for her?

Quarter to five. "This is ridiculous!" Sam roared. "Management has no right to request a copy of the minutes of union meetings. No right whatsoever! I'll go to the national on this if I have to...."

A voice emerged through the intercom speaker above the door: "Mr. Moore? There's a call for you on line two."

A gust of joy swept through him, but it was abruptly tempered by the thought that the call might be from someone else. Bracing himself for disappointment, he crossed to the counter, took a deep breath, depressed the flashing button on the phone and lifted the receiver. "Owen Moore speaking."

"You don't know me," came an unfamiliar woman's voice. "I don't know you, either."

What should have been an unpromising opening struck Owen as auspicious. A strange woman calling him. It could mean anything. He stared out through the rain-streaked window and tried to keep his optimism from bubbling over. "Yes?" he said impassively.

"My name is Nancy Burdette. I'm an attorney with Shoup, Hawley in Manhattan. I'm calling for Gillian Chappell."

He forced himself not to clutch the phone too hard. He didn't want Gillian's father to know how keyed up he was. "I see."

"You're not alone right now, are you," Nancy Burdette surmised from his terse comments.

"No, I'm not."

"Okay. I understand. I'll phrase things accordingly."

"Thanks."

"None of this makes sense, you know. This whole thing is nuts."

He laughed faintly. "I know."

"Gillian said she didn't want to call you herself because everybody at Sandifer from the receptionist on up knows her and she doesn't want her father to know she's talking to you."

"I see."

"She's my best friend, Mr. Moore. She told me a little about you—but not enough to stifle my doubts. She said she met you in Italy two years ago. But I was with her in Italy and I don't remember you."

"Well, what can I say?"

"Not much, obviously." Nancy Burdette sighed, sounding exasperated. "Just last night she was ranting and raving about what a heartless businessman you are and now she's got me playing the go-between, and I don't even know what the hell this whole thing is about."

"It's nothing I can go into right now."

"Yeah, sure. She was all alone when she called me, and it was nothing she could go into, either." Nancy mumbled something off-color under her breath. "Okay. She said to tell you she's going to this barbecue at her Aunt Lettie's house tonight and there's nothing either you or she can do about it—"

"What about tomorrow?"

Nancy sighed again. "She said maybe she'll meet you someplace. She has to think about it. She wants to know where you're staying, so she can contact you, if she decides she wants to see you."

He told her the name of the hotel, then glanced over his shoulder at Sam Chappell, who appeared to be absorbed in the document outlining layoff procedures.

"Okay," Nancy said slowly, as if she'd been writing down the hotel's name.

"Tonight," he said carefully, never letting his awareness of Sam let up.

"What about tonight?"

"Can you give me the address?"

"Her Aunt Lettie's address, you mean?"

"Yes."

A long silence stretched between him and Gillian's friend. "She didn't say I could tell you that."

"I think you should. I think it could make all the difference in the world."

"All what difference? I know, I know—you aren't alone, you can't talk. This whole thing is screwy. To tell you the truth, I don't want to be in the middle of it."

"It's too late. You already are."

"Yeah, yeah, I know." Nancy ruminated for a minute. "Look, it's not like I'm trying to be difficult, Mr. Moore, but Gillian didn't give me permission to pass along her aunt's address."

"Did she say not to?"

"Well . . . not in so many words, no."

"Show some initiative then."

Another long pause. "Maybe I should check with her first," Nancy hedged.

"I'm going to be leaving here soon. I need to know now." When Nancy still didn't leap to answer, he added, "Please."

With a groan, Nancy provided an address in Maplewood. Owen memorized it; he couldn't very well jot it down in Sam Chappell's presence. "I hope I didn't just make the biggest mistake in my life," she added.

"Hey, we all make mistakes sometimes," Owen said. Sam's attention flickered toward him, and he turned back to the window. "On the other hand, sometimes mistakes are strokes of genius in disguise. In any case, thank you."

"Gillian's probably going to boil me in oil."

"She's going to thank you. I've got to go."

"Yeah." After one final resigned sigh, Nancy said, "Listen, Mr. Moore, I don't understand any of this. But I want you to know, Gillian is very special to me."

"To me, too."

"You do anything to hurt her and I swear I'll kill you. Is that clear?"

"Absolutely."

"All right. Goodbye, Mr. Moore."

"Goodbye." He lowered the receiver into the cradle and let out a long breath. Outside the window the rain was letting up; the clouds were beginning to thin, allowing him random glimpses of blue sky. Behind him Gillian's father sat, ruffling papers and muttering under his breath, no doubt casting aspersions on Owen and everything he stood for.

Owen didn't care. He was going to see Gillian. And nothing could stop him.

GILLIAN COMMANDED HER computer to print out the data she'd amassed on Moore Enterprises. She wanted to believe the Sandifer employees would remain safe, well paid and happy under the ownership of Moore Enterprises. Yet everything she'd ever heard told her that that wouldn't happen. After Aunt Lettie's barbecue, she would go home, curl up in bed and go over all the material she'd accumulated on Owen's business. Then she'd have a clearer idea of what to think.

As if thinking were a real option.

Lord help her, she couldn't think. Couldn't concentrate. Couldn't focus. She'd been sitting at her desk for the past few hours, going through the motions of reading the depositions while her mind was somewhere else, floating through the air as soft and puffy as the shapeless clouds scattered across the sky. She'd drifted, dreamed, closed her eyes and felt Owen's lips on hers. Felt his hand on her arm. Felt his dark, dark eyes boring into her, seeking her soul, seeing everything inside it.

How had he found her?

Voices in a refrigerator.

She chuckled, but she wasn't particularly amused. If her mystery lover from Verona had to invade her life once more, why did he have to do so as the head of Moore Enterprises? Why couldn't he have been an environmental scientist, or a photographer, or a circus clown? Why did he have to be the archenemy of working people all over the country?

And why, given that he *was* their archenemy, did she have to feel as overwhelming an attraction to him now as she had two years ago?

She would figure it all out tonight. Alone in her house, in her bed, she would do her best to think, really think the whole thing through.

Tomorrow she'd have a better idea of how to cope with Owen.

THE LAST PERSON HE expected to find sipping a martini in the hotel's cocktail lounge was Ben Voltz.

"What the hell are you doing here?" Owen asked, dropping his briefcase onto the chair next to Ben's and glowering at the older man.

"I'm having a drink. Sit down, Owen. Order something for yourself."

"I can't." It was already closing in on six o'clock. He had to shower, change his clothes and set out for Maplewood.

"Sit," Ben commanded, pushing Owen's briefcase onto the floor and patting the chair. "I want to hear how things went at Sandifer Chemicals."

Reluctantly Owen took a seat. Ben was in New Jersey for a reason. The sooner Owen learned what it was, the better.

"Things went fine," he said. "Don't tell me you came here to check up on me."

"Well...yes and no. You and I have business in New York, and I thought, why not stay at the hotel Owen's staying at? Sure, it's a little out of the way, but we can just scoot across the river and be on Wall Street in minutes. Over dinner I'll tell you what I've got in mind. Do you want to freshen up first?"

"Yes, I want to freshen up—and no, you won't tell me over dinner. I've already got plans for the evening."

Ben's eyebrows twitched up. "My, my. You operate fast."

"It's not an operation. I'm...seeing an old friend. So can we make this quick?"

Ben scooped a handful of peanuts from the glass bowl on the table in front of him and popped them one at a time into his mouth, deliberately testing Owen's patience. *No,* his leisurely movements seemed to say, *we can't make this quick.*

Owen jiggled his foot and counted to twenty. He owed Ben a few minutes at the very least. Ben had been a friend to him over the years, sometimes a surrogate father. Even when they'd crossed swords over Moore Enterprises' strategies, Ben had always given Owen his respectful attention. Now it was Owen's turn to show some respect.

He tried not to glance at his watch as Ben, reed thin in his Armani suit, with his mile-high forehead and his tasseled loafers, chewed a peanut thoroughly and rinsed it down with a sip of his martini. "Your mother and Marc want you to overhaul the employee contracts at Sandifer," he said.

"That's out of the question."

"They want the union gone."

Owen shook his head. "I just spent the entire day convincing the shop steward to accept our new employment package. I'm not going to start all over again."

"His name," Ben drawled, rolling a peanut between his thumb and forefinger, "is Sam Chappell, and he's not going to accept anything. He's a known trouble-maker. I've been talking to people, Owen. I've found out about him. He's a hothead."

"The best way to cool him off is to treat the workers fairly," Owen argued. "I think we found a lot of common ground today."

"Don't be naive, Owen. According to our sources, Sam Chappell isn't the sort of person who's willing to share common ground with management. I wish we'd uncovered this material sooner, but we haven't got a strong network of contacts on the East Coast."

"What material have you uncovered?" Owen asked, his mild tone disguising his apprehension.

"Trouble at an oil refinery down the turnpike in Elizabeth. Sam Chappell and his two brothers were behind it, but Sam was the ringleader. There were several episodes—minor irritations that he blew into major altercations, the worst being a wildcat walkout over the placement of a water cooler or some such crap. Even the national refused to back him at that point. There was lots of bad blood, and during the next period of layoffs Chappell got the axe. He went to Sandifer and immediately took over the local there."

"I'm sure it wasn't a takeover. He was elected by the workers. From what I could see, he speaks for them and he has their loyalty."

"From what you could see . . ." Ben snorted disdainfully. "You think he'd let the new boss man see if he had no backing? The guy craves power, Owen. If you're planning to make a go of it with Sandifer Chemicals, Sam Chappell has to disappear."

Owen offered a deceptively benign smile. He refused to let Ben rattle him. If Sam Chappell was a problem, he was a problem. He was also Gillian's father, and Owen wasn't going to condemn the man without concrete evidence.

"I'm running Moore Enterprises now, Ben. And I don't care how much Chappell craves power. I'm the one who decides how we're going to deal with him. Not you, not Marc and not my mother."

"Owen—"

"If they sent you all the way across the country to twist my arm, Ben, I'm sorry. You made a long trip for nothing."

"I didn't make a long trip for nothing," Ben insisted. "We really do have business in New York. If you're going to be buying manufacturing concerns on the East Coast, you need to line up some people in the region whom you can work through, a New York-based investment banker and so on. I've got appointments to meet with a few people who come highly recommended. I want you to participate in those meetings."

"Sure." As irritating as Ben's paternalistic attitude could be, Owen was honest enough to recognize the wisdom of Ben's experience in certain areas. Owen would never have thought of finding a banker on the East Coast, an expert familiar with the local scene.

Ben leaned back in his chair, his drink cradled in his hands and his bald spot glistening where the overhead light hit it. His smile was warm yet shadowed, as if he didn't quite trust Owen. "It's always such a pleasant surprise when you agree to do something I tell you to do."

Owen returned the older man's guarded smile. "I'm not a kid, Ben. I'm thirty years old, I've got a business degree and I've pulled off a few successful ventures of my own. I don't think it's naive to find peaceful solutions to problems. Sometimes it's even beneficial."

"It's also a way of kicking your poor old father in the teeth."

"I do things the way I do them because it's right, not because I want to hurt my father."

"You ran off to Italy to hurt your father."

"I ran off because I couldn't coexist with him. But I've gotten along just fine doing business my own way, Ben. I took the reins at Moore Enterprises because my father asked me to. If he wants me to keep running the company, I will. If he wants to get rid of me, I'm gone. But I'm not going to change my philosophy—not for him, not for you, and not because you've heard Sam Chappell is a hothead."

The dim, smoky atmosphere of the cocktail lounge emphasized the pouches under Ben's eyes and the creases at the corners of his mouth. "You're a hothead, too," he accused. "I don't want you going off half-cocked and making a fool of yourself."

"Don't worry about it."

"I can't help but worry. Neither can your father. It's just the way we are."

Despite his resentment, Owen was touched. He and his father were so often at each other's throats and Ben was so often running interference between them, Owen sometimes forgot that underlying all their squabbles and disagreements was a deep, abiding affection.

He reached across the seat and patted Ben's shoulder. "I'll be as coolheaded as I can. And now, I've really got to run."

"This 'old friend'..." Ben winked. "How old is she?"

Owen grinned. "Exactly the right age."

"Can I have breakfast with you, at least? Or have you got plans for that, too?"

"Sure, I'll have breakfast with you."

"I'm in Room 806. Buzz me when you wake up."

After a farewell handshake, Owen rose and strolled to the elevator, anxious to put everything out of his mind—Ben's warnings about Sam Chappell, his doting, and his unexpected, not altogether welcome presence in New Jersey.

To have breakfast with Ben tomorrow meant Owen couldn't spend the night with Gillian.

As if that had ever been a possibility.

Gillian was far more likely to hate him for showing up at her aunt's barbecue than to invite him to stay long enough to have breakfast with her. She'd told him not to come tonight. She had implied she wasn't ready to deal with him yet.

But he couldn't stay away. He had to see her—if not alone, then with her family. If not at her home or his hotel, at someone else's house.

He didn't care. He would crash the barbecue and risk her wrath. He would do whatever he had to do to see her.

And as angry as she might be, as indignant, as enraged…she would be glad he came. She would want to be with him as much as he wanted to be with her. She wouldn't be able to help herself any more than he could help himself.

They'd touched the statue, after all.

Chapter Six

"Gillian! It's about time. I thought you'd be here sooner."

Gillian smiled and allowed Aunt Lettie to sweep her into the house and smother her in a hug. Gillian was several inches taller than her aunt, and she'd been an adult for quite some time, but Lettie always had a way of making her feel like a little girl.

No doubt that was because she *had* been a little girl with Lettie. Gillian had been four years old when her mother had died and her father had turned to his brother Charlie and sister-in-law Letitia for help. Each morning before sunrise, her father had driven her to Charlie and Lettie's crowded little Cape Cod house, leaving her in the company of her plump, effusive aunt and her red-faced, squalling cousins, and then returned to pick her up late at night. Gillian remembered Lettie's tenacious efforts to coax a smile from her, to bring her out of her misery.

Gillian had felt so old when her mother died, but with patience and love, Lettie had turned her back into the little girl she was supposed to be. When Gillian began kindergarten, Lettie used to drive all the way to the grade school in Irvington to pick her up each day after class, because the school bus wouldn't drop her off in Maplewood. Lettie took her shopping for dresses, gave her haircuts in the homey, brightly lit kitchen, helped her with science projects and drilled her on her spelling lessons.

To this day, Gillian resented the forces that had deprived her of a mother at so young an age. But while Lettie could never replace her mother, Gillian had grown to love her just as dearly.

"Everyone's been here for a while," Lettie said, ushering Gillian through the parlor and into the kitchen. "It's after seven-thirty. We wanted to wait with dinner till you got here, but Charlie Junior started complaining about missing the game, so I told people to go ahead and eat. Charlie, put two burgers on for Gillian, okay?" she shouted through a window to her husband, who was holding forth outside on the deck, reciting one of his long-winded traveling-salesman jokes to a young man Gillian had never seen before.

"Who's the guy?" she asked Lettie. "Amy's new boyfriend?"

"Amy has five new boyfriends, and she won't let us meet any of them," Lettie grumbled. "I don't know what it is with you two—she dates too much and you date too little."

"I don't date too little," Gillian argued, plucking an olive from the bowl of coleslaw on the counter and popping it into her mouth. The last thing she wanted to discuss tonight was her social life. As long as Owen was in New Jersey—as long as he was on the planet—she wouldn't consider that a safe subject.

She crossed the room to the refrigerator and opened it in search of a soft drink. The motor clicked on and hummed, but she didn't hear any voices emerging from the crowded shelves or the cold white walls. She took comfort in the possibility that she wasn't quite as demented as Owen was.

"So, why are you late?" Lettie asked. "Working too hard, as usual?"

Gillian grabbed a can of soda, closed the refrigerator and turned to her aunt with a sheepish smile. "Working too hard, as usual," she confirmed, refusing to admit the real reason she was late: she'd been distracted, rattled, too disturbed to function efficiently. She'd almost gotten lost on her way home and she'd braked at a green light not once but twice. She'd changed clothes twice and she'd spent a good fifteen minutes staring at her mail without reading any of it.

She'd stared at the folder of information she'd accrued on Moore Enterprises, too. Stared at it and thought, *He's in New Jersey. He knows where I am. He hasn't been involved with a woman in two years, because he touched the statue.*

And now, belatedly, she was in the old familiar kitchen in Maplewood listening to her aunt nag her about her paltry social life, when the reason for its paltriness was right that very minute in a hotel room no more than ten miles away.

Or else the reason was in Verona, Italy, in a brick courtyard with ivy growing up the walls.

"Hi, sweetie." Uncle Charlie sidled up to the open kitchen window and peered into the kitchen. Although his face was shadowed, she knew it well enough to fill in what she couldn't see: the fringe of thinning hair, the bushy eyebrows, the broad nose and infectious smile. "How's life in the law business?"

"Litigious," she reported as she popped open the can and took a sip.

"How do you want these burgers cooked? Medium?"

"She'll come outside and tell you," Lettie interjected.

Gillian frowned. Why couldn't she just tell her uncle through the screen?

Uncle Charlie vanished from the window and she directed her frown to Lettie. "Go on out," Lettie answered her unasked question. "Enjoy the evening."

"I haven't even said hello to my father yet, or any of the others."

"They're all in the den, arguing over who was a better player in his prime, Magic Johnson or Larry Bird."

Gillian rolled her eyes. "They've been having that fight for twelve years."

"And they'll still be having it twelve years from now. Spare yourself, honey. Go outside and keep your uncle company."

Gillian suspected her aunt had an ulterior motive for remanding her to the deck. As soon as she stepped outside she understood what it was.

The man her uncle had been regaling with his time-worn jokes pushed away from the deck's railing, where he'd been lounging, and presented her with a friendly smile. He was a pleasant-looking fellow, with dark blond hair and a tidy mustache underlining a thick, sturdy nose. His eyes were blue, his cheeks dimpled and his right hand extended. "You must be Gillian," he said.

Her aunt's critique of her inadequate social life echoed inside her. She gazed at the handsome man in his meticulously casual attire and heard the clanks and whirs of matchmaking machinery. "I am Gillian," she said carefully.

Whatever vague intuition she was harboring came into sharp focus when Uncle Charlie handed her his spatula and said, "Here, Gillian—would you keep an eye on those burgers? I've got to go inside."

Sending her uncle a desperate look that he chose to ignore, she took the spatula and moved cautiously to the gas grill, where two burgers were sizzling. She heard the screen door clap shut and realized that she was alone with this amiable stranger and very much the object of his attention.

"Your uncle isn't exactly subtle, is he?" he said.

Gillian looked at him. He resumed his place by the railing, leaning his hips against the pressurized wood, his arms folded across his chest and his smile indulgent.

She felt it incumbent upon her to return his smile. "Who are you?"

"Perry Royerson. And don't blame your uncle. It was your father's idea to invite me to this barbecue."

"And now he's hiding in the den," she muttered, although Perry's genial attitude made it impossible for her to remain irritated. "I'm sorry they put you up to this."

"I'm not," he said. At her quick glance, he added, "Your aunt's potato salad is fantastic."

"You've eaten already?"

"Just a little. I'll have one of those burgers, though, so you won't have to eat alone."

He seemed nice. And he was unquestionably handsome. "How do you know my father?"

"I'm a pediatrician at his medical center."

"A pediatrician?" A surprised laugh escaped her. "Do I have a baby brother I don't know about?"

Perry chuckled and shook his head. "His truck was parked next to my car outside the building when a dead branch fell and landed on our hoods. We both came out at the same time, helped each other clean off our vehicles and check for scratches, and..." he shrugged "...one thing led to another."

Gillian eyed him dubiously. "What do you mean, one thing led to another?"

"Your father's as subtle as your uncle. He asked me if I was single, and when I told him I was he sang the praises of his wonderful daughter, the lawyer."

"Oh, God," she groaned, her cheeks darkening in embarrassment.

"At first I was skeptical. But then he pulled out a picture of you that he carries in his wallet, and I decided it was worth a weeknight of my life to see if you were as pretty in person as you were in the photo."

"Thanks." She refused to take his compliment too seriously. "That photo is about five years old."

"And it doesn't do you justice."

She fell silent. She detected nothing phony in Perry's flattery, nothing pushy. He seriously seemed to think she was pretty. She really ought to give him a chance. He was handsome, charming, a pediatrician, tolerant of her father...Perry Royerson had a hell of a lot going for him.

But it wasn't enough. It would never be enough, not as long as she was fixated on Owen Moore.

She poked at the edges of the broiling hamburgers with the spatula and tried to work through her thoughts. She ought to tell Perry that, despite his many fine attributes, she simply couldn't encourage his interest. But then he would ask why, and she would have to tell him...

Tell him what? That for the past two years she'd been carrying a torch for a rich man looking for fun, a premier thug in the business world, a man whose last name she hadn't even known until a few hours ago—and now that she did know, she was sick about it?

With a sigh, she flipped the burgers and lifted two paper plates from the stack beside the grill. Beyond the chain-link fence bordering the neighborhood playground that abutted her aunt's backyard, she saw someone strolling down the street toward the gate.

"Here's your burger," she said, handing Perry a plate. "Should we go in? The game is going to start any minute."

"Why don't we eat out here? Everything smells so nice and clean after the rain."

Sure, everything smelled nice and clean, but she understood his suggestion for what it was: a way to spend a little more time alone with her. Again she contemplated telling him she wasn't interested in forging a relationship with him. But to insist that they join her noisy, scrappy family inside, when she, too, would rather enjoy the balmy evening, didn't make sense.

Reluctantly, she dabbed some ketchup onto her burger and took a seat on one of the plastic-cushioned deck chairs. Perry remained slouched comfortably against the railing, his plate balanced in his hands.

Not wanting to be rude, she asked him about his work as a pediatrician. What he had to say was no doubt fascinating, but her mind wandered. In the light radiating from a fixture above the back door, she noticed residual raindrops sparkling on the leaves of the red maple beyond the deck and glinting in the grass. Through the open kitchen window she heard voices, laughter, bellicose predictions about whether the New Jersey Nets would ever be champions. Her gaze followed the twin headlight beams of a car cruising slowly down the street, its windows open and its radio blaring rock music. Then her vision snagged on the teenager in the playground.

He wasn't a teenager, she realized. He was a man. He loitered near the swings, then moseyed toward the fence that separated a playground from Lettie and Charlie's backyard.

Owen.

Even in shadow—especially in shadow—she recognized him. She didn't know how he'd found her aunt and uncle's house, or why he'd come. But she knew, without having to see his blazing eyes, his sensuous mouth, his strong, possessive hands...

She knew it was Owen.

"The thing is," Perry was saying, "while it breaks your heart when a child gets sick, as a doctor you always feel you can do more for children than you can for adults. Children haven't spent thirty or forty years abusing their bodies—drinking, smoking, clogging their blood vessels with cholesterol. So there's always that extra bit of hope that because they're still young and growing you can do something for them."

"Hmm," Gillian said, nodding dutifully and trying not to stare at the dark figure nearing the fence and curling his fingers through the chain-link mesh. "Excuse me, Perry—I've got to go talk to that guy."

"Who?" Perry twisted around and squinted into the fading twilight. "That vagrant?"

"I know him," Gillian explained uncertainly. "I'm just going to tell him to go away."

Perry set down his plate and started to rise. "Maybe I should come with you."

"No," she said, abruptly enough to startle him. She managed a tenuous smile. "It's all right, Perry. He isn't dangerous. I'll just find out what he wants and tell him to leave."

She didn't have to descend the deck stairs and walk past the red maple, past Aunt Lettie's small vegetable garden and across the damp grass to the fence to find out what Owen wanted. She knew. He'd never done anything to conceal what he wanted.

I want you. Even more now than two years ago.

She also knew how much good telling him to leave would do. He wouldn't leave until he got what he wanted.

I want you.

He didn't move as she approached. He made no attempt either to scale the fence or backtrack to the gate. In the diffuse light of a mist-shrouded crescent moon, she saw his lips curve in a smile. He looked not surprised, not smug, but simply happy, as if fate had ordained that she would stroll across the lawn to him, that he would be there waiting for her, that her hands would find his through the fence, that she would hook her fingers through linked wires as he had so that their hands were touching.

She wished she could feel angry, or delighted. Her emotions were tangled, though. Anger and delight were there, but so were anxiety and arousal and a strange helplessness that she would never escape Owen, never get over him, never have her old, normal, even-keeled life back.

"Did your voices tell you where I'd be?" she asked.

"Actually, it was one of *your* voices. I believe her name was Nancy Burdette."

"Nancy told you?" Gillian was careful to speak in a near whisper, but her shock and indignation were audible in the harsh rasp of her breath. "I can't believe it! The traitor!"

"Don't blame her," Owen murmured. She could feel more than see his amused and confident grin. His fingers flexed against hers through the fence; the open wire links did nothing to protect her from his potent allure.

"Why would she tell you where I'd be? I needed some time away from you, to think about what happened today."

"She told me because I twisted her arm," Owen answered. "And if you want to think about what happened today, go right ahead. I won't stop you."

He wouldn't stop her from walking away from the playground and returning to the house, either. He wouldn't stop her from withdrawing her hands from the fence, turning her back on him, and spending the rest of the evening exchanging small talk with Perry Royerson, or joining the rest of her family for some cheering and booing over the televised basketball game.

He wouldn't stop her. She would stop herself. And he knew it.

Around them the air reverberated with a night chorus of crickets. A light breeze ruffled the leaves of a sycamore, jarring loose a few leftover raindrops which spattered onto her hair. From what sounded like a great distance, she heard Perry Royerson call to her, "Gillian? Is everything all right?"

"Everything's fine," she called back, unsure of whether that was the truth.

"Is he your brother?" Owen asked.

She shook her head. "I haven't got a brother. He's an eligible bachelor. My father and my aunt are trying to set me up with him."

Owen glanced past her at the tall blond man watching them from the deck. "Should I be concerned?"

"Yes," Gillian said, even though Perry posed no threat to him. "He's a very nice man. A doctor. A pediatrician."

"Ah. That's much more respectable than a corporate-takeover artist."

"It is."

He smiled. Against her better judgment, she smiled back. "Let me come in," he said.

Her fingers tightened around the fence's links. Owen slid his hands over hers, covering her knuckles. The contact of his thick, hard skin against hers sent sizzles of sensation up her arms.

She needed to be alone. She needed to think things through, figure things out. She needed to keep her distance from Owen. Yet if the fence hadn't stood between them she would be in his arms right now. She wondered if he knew that.

"You can't come in," she whispered, hearing a quiver in her voice. "My father is there. He hates you, Owen."

"I can win him over."

That smile again, confident, almost arrogant. "I doubt it," she argued. Owen hadn't even won *her* over.

"Come on, invite me in. I won't talk shop. I'll just be a pleasant party guest."

"You don't understand. My father *hates* you. He hates everything you stand for. He doesn't trust you. You're the antithesis of everything he believes in."

"The devil incarnate, huh?"

"Something like that."

Owen's smile didn't waver. "He struck me as a reasonable man. We can find some areas of agreement, don't you think?"

She shook her head. "I don't even know how to tell him I know you, let alone that you and I..." She didn't dare to finish the thought.

Owen finished it for her. "That you and I have kissed?"

She was grateful to him for not taking it further and speaking the whole truth: that she and Owen craved each other heedlessly, recklessly, like an addict craves his drug. The news that she had kissed Owen would probably be enough to send her father into paroxysms of rage.

"It's not that my father controls me," she clarified, her voice still low, competing with the occasional purr of a car coasting past the playground and the incessant chirping of the crickets. "But he and I are close. We depend on each other. We keep each other going. We're a team, Owen. We're family. I can't explain it—"

"You don't have to explain," Owen said, his smile finally fading and his tone earnest. His thumb stroked hers again, gently, circling the silver wires of the fence and imparting less longing than compassion. "He's your father."

His gaze flickered past her again and she turned to see Perry marching down the deck stairs to the yard. Her mind ran a quick comparison of the two men: Perry was an inch or so taller than Owen and a bit beefy in contrast to Owen's lean, wiry build. Perry wore a short-sleeved shirt of madras plaid and tailored khaki trousers; Owen had on a shirt of loose-fitting linen, with the sleeves rolled up to his elbows, and snug blue jeans. Perry exuded respectability. Owen exuded sexuality.

"What's going on?" Perry asked with deceptive nonchalance. "Is this fellow causing problems?"

More than you can imagine, Gillian wanted to reply. "No. We were just—" she let her hands drop from the fence as Perry drew close "—talking."

Perry eyed Owen suspiciously, then peered down at Gillian. He seemed uncertain of his rights and responsibilities in this situation. "Are you ready to go in now?" he asked her. "The game's in full swing."

Gillian bit her lip. The NBA play-offs held no appeal for her. She would rather stand across a high fence from Owen, arguing or whispering secrets, or not speaking at all, simply weaving her fingers through the fence, through his. But to tell Perry to go away and leave her with Owen would probably ignite a crisis.

Before she could think of what to say, Owen nodded at Perry. "I didn't mean to keep her from the game," he said. "I'd better be moving on. Will I see you later?"

No.

Of course.

"I don't know," she said.

"You know how to reach me."

He pivoted and sauntered in long, graceful strides across the playground, sidestepping the swings and then the slide. *Coward,* she scolded herself. *Tell him to come back. Invite him to join you inside.*

Perry arched his arm loosely around her shoulders. "Strange guy, wasn't he?" he commented, ushering her back to the house.

"He is kind of strange," she conceded.

The farther they walked from the fence, the more weary she felt, as if Owen had stolen the energy from her. It was stupid, foolish, totally unjustifiable, but she wanted nothing but to break from Perry and race after

Owen, to run off with him, to forget her father and Lettie and Charlie and the play-off game and just be with Owen, and damn the consequences.

Instead, she dragged one foot in front of the other across the soft, fragrant grass, around the red maple and up the steps. She let Perry keep his arm draped across her shoulders, felt the starchy cotton of his shirt against her elbow, filled her lungs with the lemony scent of his after-shave.

At the top step, she shot a quick glance over her shoulder. Owen stood near the playground gate, a mere sliver of darkness on the edge of the light funneling down from a street lamp. He stood perfectly still.

He was watching her, she knew. Watching as she and Perry moved into the light of the deck, Perry's arm still around her.

She should have brought him in, should have told her father the truth—that Owen was her passion, her obsession, the sum and substance of her dreams over the past two years. But she lacked the nerve. She wanted to avoid the confrontation. Perhaps Owen would never forgive her for refusing him entry into this gathering of her family.

Maybe, by the time she called Nancy to figure out how to reach him, Owen would no longer want to be reached.

Chapter Seven

"That gentleman..." Romeo observed the scene below. "The physician. He reminds me of someone."

Juliet smiled wistfully. "Paris," she said.

"Paris? We never were to the city of lights and lovers, Juliet."

"No, my lord—the gentleman reminds you of Count Paris, my betrothed. The nobleman my parents wished for me to marry."

Romeo's befuddlement waned. "Ah, yes. Paris. I slew him."

"You slew many people, dear husband. You were so terribly quick to draw your sword."

"He challenged me," Romeo defended himself. "At your tomb. He drew first. He called me vile—and even at that I would not have killed him if he had not come at me."

"He made mistakes," Juliet conceded, "as did we all. And like you and me, poor Paris paid for those mistakes with his life. He was a good man, Romeo. He loved me dearly."

"Not as dearly as I did."

This she did not contest. Nobody loved her as dearly as Romeo, nor did she love anyone as dearly as she

*loved him. Had she not met Romeo, not fallen in love
with him and married him in secret, she might have accepted Paris as a husband. He had been rich, well connected, respectful to her parents and devoted to her. He
would have made a fine bridegroom, had she but loved
him.*

*But she had loved only Romeo. Even though he was
not a kinsman of the prince, even though he was not an
intimate of her parents, she had loved him.*

*Loving Paris would have been easier, but love wasn't
always easy. It followed its own logic—or illogic. Reason mattered little.*

*"I wonder if the physician, Perry Royerson, might
love our Gillian,"* she murmured.

"Do not wish for it," Romeo warned. *"He seems a
pleasant enough fellow, and Owen has indicated a certain impulsiveness of character. We would not like to see
this American stage strewn with bodies."*

*Juliet pondered the possibilities. "Our friends below
are older than we were at the time our drama unfolded.
Perhaps they are more temperate. They move about
their world unarmed."*

*"Even so, they have the power within them to wound,
to hurt with a pain as deep as death,"* Romeo warned.
*"Passion is a weapon no less cruel than any other. One
needs not a sword or saber to inflict agonies. One needs
only emotion—love, hatred, envy, unthinking rage.
Had we lived today, Juliet, I should not have slain Tybalt, or Paris, or myself. Yet many people would have
been hurt. That is a regrettable fact of love."*

*Juliet gazed admiringly at Romeo. How she adored
this side of him, his sensitive, concerned, philosophical
aspect. Centuries ago, when she and he had first fallen
in love, he had been too swift to anger, too hasty to*

judge and misjudge. Yet his acts had been executed out of abiding compassion. He hadn't intended to fight Tybalt, but he'd been coerced into it. And he hadn't wanted to fight Paris, either. He had tried to send him away before they came to blows. All he had done was to ask Paris to leave Juliet's tomb.

As well he'd had a right. He, after all, had been her true husband. "How I love you, Romeo," she sighed.

"And I you," he whispered. "Do Gillian and Owen love each other as much as we do?"

"They will have to—at least as much—if they are to escape a sad ending."

"And," Romeo added, "if they are to avoid Gillian's choosing the sensible partner over the impossible love. Dr. Royerson is well suited and has been promoted by her family. If only she had married Owen first, just as you had married me. You could never seriously contemplate Paris as a husband, because you already had a husband."

"That we were married only added a degree of complication to what was in truth a simple matter—I loved you and no one but you." She mulled over Romeo's statement. "Do you believe the love between Gillian and Owen is impossible?"

"I am not yet sure it is love," Romeo asserted. "They have talked greatly of wants and needs, but not of love."

"Because they are afraid," said Juliet. "Because to speak the word love is a frightening thing, so they call it by other names. But what's in a name? Love by any other name is still love."

Romeo laughed. "I could not have said it better myself."

HE HAD NO IDEA where he was.

He'd been driving for an hour, in long, looping circuits, up and down highways, on and off exit ramps. For some reason, the map the hotel's concierge had given him was incomprehensible. He stared at it and saw only Gillian—and that man with his arm around her.

He was tired. Edgy. Disturbed that she'd backed off from him, that she'd let that big, blond chump touch her, that he and not Owen had gotten to spend the evening with her.

When was he going to regain his sanity? How had he become so preoccupied with Gillian that he couldn't even decipher a road map?

Why had he wound up standing in that accursed courtyard in Verona one afternoon two years ago? Why had Gillian let her friend talk her into touching the statue? Why had her eyes met his the instant her hand had brushed against the bronze? Of all the people in the universe, why had this madness chosen him and Gillian?

Swearing under his breath, he drove down a road away from the highway, in search of civilization. A service station, a coffee shop—someplace where a kindly patron could tell him how the hell to get back to his hotel.

The road cut a straight line past neat middle-class houses landscaped with dewy lawns, flowering shrubs and stately trees. Up ahead he saw signs of life—a traffic light and some neon indicating a commercial zone. The first open establishment he came to was a bar.

He parked the rental car, tossed the useless map aside and got out. The night air was mild, the last traces of the day's drizzle evaporated by a brisk, dry breeze. He shoved his hands through his hair, observed as the traffic light ran its familiar pattern from red to green to yellow to red, and smiled. He was feeling a little less disoriented.

Until he entered the bar.

It was a typical joint, dimly lit, populated mostly by men. A television above the bar broadcast the basketball play-off game; at the rear, where the customers sat at tables, a jukebox blasted an old Doobie Brothers hit.

Owen sidled up to the bar, turned to the fellow on the stool next to him, and asked, "What town is this?"

"Verona."

He must have misheard, or misunderstood. The babble from the television and the blaring rock music must have distorted the man's voice. He was thickset, with bulbous lips; maybe he had a speech impediment. Possibly he was drunk.

"Excuse me?" Owen asked.

"You're in Verona. Ve-ro-na," he enunciated in response to Owen's obvious confusion.

Owen closed his eyes and turned away. It was a dream, a bad dream. He was lost in suburban northern New Jersey, and a stranger, a barfly he'd never seen before, was trying to convince him he was in Verona.

The bartender approached and Owen ordered a beer. Either it would clear his brain or completely fog it. Whichever result it got would be an improvement over his current state of limbo about whether he was in America or Italy, whether he was in reality or fantasy.

How had he reached this place?

He nursed his beer and tried to sort it out. He'd had no trouble locating Gillian's aunt's house earlier that evening. He had driven to Maplewood, asked for directions at a gas station, and wended his way to the playground the attendant had identified as a neighborhood landmark. It had been so simple. He'd found the street, the house, Gillian.

She'd seemed happy that he'd found her, too—or, if not happy, at least accepting of it in some deep, indefinable way. She'd twisted her fingers through the fence to reach him, and they'd stood there, the woven wire mesh between them, murmuring, touching, communicating. Despite the fence, they'd been together.

If only one of them had had the nerve to climb over to the other side.

But then the blond guy with the mustache had come over, polite but proprietary, placing his arm around Gillian as if to say, *You're on that side and we're on this side. I'm with her and you're not.*

Owen told himself not to let the existence of the blond man bother him. He'd been with women over the past couple of years, and nothing had come of it. Nothing would come of Gillian and her blond friend, either.

But knowing that didn't make it any easier for Owen to acknowledge the fact that the other guy had gotten to put his arm around her tonight and enter the house with her and be with her, while Owen was stranded in a dark, beery-smelling tavern that some clown had just told him was in Verona.

He wasn't jealous. Jealousy simply wasn't an emotion he indulged in. He hadn't been jealous when Rosalie married someone else. He'd been thrilled for her and pleased to welcome her husband into his circle of friends.

Even before Gillian, he'd never been jealous. He'd fought for what he believed in; he'd lost his temper over his father's questionable business ethics. But while he wished some things in his life were different, he never wasted time lusting for what others had. Instead, he focused on figuring out what he wanted and going after it, whether it was a specialty chemical company or a woman.

His beer bottle still nearly full, he pulled a few dollars from his wallet. The bartender hurried over. "Anything wrong?" he asked, looking at the scarcely touched drink.

"I guess I'm just not that thirsty," Owen explained. "By the way, what town am I in?"

The bartender's eyes narrowed on Owen. "Look, buddy, you want me to call you a cab?"

"No. I'm not drunk. I had two sips."

"Yeah, right. And you're getting ready to pay and walk out without finishing the bottle. And you don't know where you are. Kind of adds up, don't you think?"

"I'm from California," Owen insisted. It dawned on him that, as sober as he was, he wasn't coming across as sane. Anxious not to be hauled off to some detox center or holding cell, he opened his wallet once more and pulled out his California driver's license. "I don't live around here. I don't know the area. I had an appointment in Maplewood and now I'm trying to find my way back to my hotel in Fort Lee."

"Fort Lee? You sure didn't take the direct route, pal. How'd you wind up here?"

"I wish I knew."

"All right," the bartender said, apparently convinced that Owen wasn't drunk. He rattled off some directions. "Have you got that?"

Owen didn't have a damned thing except his pride, and he wasn't about to sacrifice that by asking the bartender to repeat what he'd said. "I think so. Thanks."

"No problem. Two-eighty to I-95. You'll see—it's as easy as pie."

"Right." Owen remembered the time his sister had tried to teach him how to make a blueberry pie. The experience had given him an entirely new understanding of the phrase "easy as pie."

He left the bar, grateful to escape the smoky, musty atmosphere. The bartender's directions registered like a foreign language, a string of syllables that failed to cohere into a meaningful statement.

He unlocked the car, slid behind the wheel, turned on the overhead light and lifted the map. Then he put it down. Who cared how he was going to get back to the hotel? He was in Verona.

Verona.

He turned the ignition key and pulled away from the curb.

Forty minutes later, he discovered a sleepy block of modest ranch and Cape Cod houses lining the curbless street. He had long ago lost count of how many roads he'd driven down, how many corners he'd turned, how many other sleepy blocks he'd journeyed down.

If this was Verona, it was the most American Verona he'd ever seen. The main business district comprised one broad boulevard lined with shops—a hardware store, a sporting-goods shop, a camera store, a bakery, a realtor, a deli, an independent insurance office, a Chinese restaurant specializing in take-out, a fire department and a church featuring impressive Gothic architecture.

He'd cruised up one road and down another, searching for the *real* Verona, the Verona of narrow cobblestone alleys, brick-and-stucco buildings with long windows framed by wooden shutters, ornate but-

tresses, umbrella-shielded stalls, cottonwoods and olive trees and wall-climbing rosebushes, and rococo
statues adorning the rooftops. He'd searched for the
Verona of the *Castel Vecchio,* the *Chiesa di Santa Ma-
ria* and the *Fiume Adige,* the silver *S*-shaped river that
coursed through the city. He'd searched for the *tratto-
rias* and the *caffes,* the *mercatos* and the *pasticcerias,*
and the Arena dominating the heart of the city in ancient grandeur, just a short stroll from the courtyard
where the bronze statue of Juliet stood.

He'd found none of those things. What he'd found,
instead, was this one quiet residential lane, inter-
changeable with so many of the other quiet residential
lanes he'd driven down.

He steered to the side of the road and parked. Turning off the engine, he gazed about himself and tried to
figure out what had brought him to this street.

The same thing that had brought him to Verona—if
he was truly in Verona: magic, or dementia, or both.

Across the street and up a few houses he heard an
outer door slam shut, the loud thump echoing off the
shingled walls of the neighboring homes. He watched
through the windshield as a light came on in the broad
front window and then a figure moved into view. A
slender woman with thick, wavy hair. The light struck
it, igniting it with shimmers of gold.

Gillian.

He was crazier than he'd realized. He was seeing vi-
sions now, illusions, *de*lusions. What would Gillian be
doing here? She was in Maplewood, with her aunt and
uncle and her father and the blond guy with the mustache.

Yet the woman in the window, slim and curvaceous,
with strong shoulders and narrow hips just barely visi-

ble above the low sill…God, but she looked exactly like Gillian.

She drew the curtains, transforming herself into an amorphous shadow fractured by the rippling cloth. The light went off in the room and she vanished altogether.

A moment later she reappeared as a light came on in a smaller window at the other end of the house. Again he saw the woman's tawny, wavy hair highlighted with amber, and her trim body, her face a heart-shaped darkness against the windowpane as she peered out.

Ever since he'd left Gillian at her aunt's house—ever since he'd left her in Italy—he'd been searching for something. He wondered whether this woman was searching for something, too.

He heard the muted squeak of her window sliding open. Without knowing why, he climbed out of his car. He wasn't sure if she actually jumped slightly when he shut the car door, or if he just imagined her jumping. He couldn't tell if she'd seen him, or whether she was even looking his way.

She couldn't possibly be Gillian. Gillian was several towns to the south, in the bosom of her family, in the shelter of another man's arm.

Still, Owen couldn't tear his eyes from the woman in the window. He wanted to approach, but what would he say? How would he explain himself? He'd already been taken for a drunk in the bar. He didn't want to be taken for a Peeping Tom, too.

So he only leaned against the front bumper of his car, inhaling the smells of mown grass and blossoming azaleas, watching the silhouetted woman hover in her window for an interminable moment before she tugged a string, bringing down the pleated shades. Then she left the window. His gaze remained on her shadow as it first grew distorted and then faint and fuzzy, and then finally disappeared.

It could be a hopeful sign, he thought, continuing to observe the house until the light in the small window flickered off. For the first time since he'd arrived in New Jersey—for the first time since he'd arrived in the United States after he'd departed from Verona—he had actually spent a few minutes captivated by a woman who wasn't Gillian Chappell.

Whatever lunacy had overtaken him and lured him to this peaceful suburban village, something good had come of it. He had stopped thinking about Gillian long enough to think of a stranger in a window. A stranger with elegant shoulders like Gillian's, and a chaotic cascade of blondish-brown hair like hers, and seductively slender hips like hers. A woman who could have passed for Gillian—but *wasn't* Gillian.

Maybe the spell was beginning to dissolve. Maybe he was on the road to recovery.

Maybe someday he would actually be free of her.

GILLIAN LEFT THE WINDOW open when she closed the blind. She would check again in a few minutes to see if that man was still lurking by the car down the block. She understood the risk in leaving a ground-floor window open, yet the evening air was mild and pleasant and she preferred to sleep in a well-ventilated room.

As if she had any hope in hell of falling asleep tonight. She was so wired she couldn't imagine relaxing enough to doze off for the next several decades. She flopped across her bed and groaned. Her head throbbed and her fingers felt numb, as if the fence through which she'd clasped hands with Owen had been electrified and had burned away her ability to feel anything.

Anything other than Owen.

Why had he come after her when she'd told him flat out that she didn't want to see him tonight? Why had he gone to the playground by Charlie and Lettie's house? Why had he chased her, stalked her, found her, tried to insinuate his way into her evening, her life?

It was all Nancy's fault. Two years ago Nancy had persuaded Gillian to touch the statue, and four hours ago Nancy had told Owen where he would find Gillian tonight.

She rolled onto her stomach and reached for her bedside phone. She punched the buttons for Nancy's number, listened to the ringing on the other end, and then heard Nancy say, "Hello?"

"Don't sound so innocent," Gillian railed. "If lives were money, yours wouldn't be worth enough to keep a parking meter ticking for ten minutes."

A moment's silence on the line. "Gillian?"

"Why did you tell him where I'd be? How could you do that to me?"

"Oh." Nancy's voice wavered. "I'm sorry, I—oh, Gillian, I don't know why I told him. He asked."

"He asked. And if he'd asked you to drop a nuclear bomb on the White House, I'm sure you would have done that, too."

"He didn't seem dangerous. Why? What happened?"

"What happened? He showed up at the playground next door to Aunt Lettie's house, that's what happened."

Another silence. Evidently Nancy didn't think that sounded so very horrible. In retrospect, neither did Gillian.

"He didn't even join the gathering?"

"He wanted to," Gillian admitted. "I wouldn't let him."

"Well." Nancy's tone was stronger now, a touch sarcastic. "He showed up at a playground and didn't join your family. I can see why you want to draw and quarter me."

"It was very awkward," Gillian insisted, coiling her finger through the twisted cord and trying to hang onto her anger. "My father had brought a man to the barbecue to meet me."

"Wow. Two boys for every girl. I wish I'd been invited."

"It wasn't like that—"

"Well, look, Gillian, if you don't want them both, can I have one? Preferably the one I talked to. I'm not as put off by corporate pirates as you are. And no offense, but your father's taste in appropriate boyfriends might not jibe with mine."

"The man my father invited was very nice. Handsome, too. His name was Perry Royerson. He's a doctor."

"A handsome doctor. Hmm. Great pay, lousy hours. You can have him. I'll take the Moore guy. He doesn't need a big salary. He's probably already richer than sin."

"Probably," Gillian allowed, reminding herself that Owen's wealth was a mark against him. She was a working-class girl, and she had little affection for someone whose family had achieved prosperity on the backs of other working-class people.

Yet she couldn't bring herself to go along with Nancy's flip bantering and offer her a chance at Owen Moore. Owen was Gillian's, regardless of who he was or what he was worth.

"So, tell me about the doctor," Nancy requested. "Are you going to see him again?"

"I don't know. I gave him my phone number, but only because my father was standing there, sending me one of his looks. I kind of thought it would be rude to tell Perry I wasn't interested."

"But you aren't."

"He's very nice," Gillian insisted, wishing she could talk herself into liking him.

"All right," Nancy said, accurately gathering Gillian's true sentiments from her hesitant tone. "Don't tell me about the doctor. Tell me about Owen Moore. Is he better looking than the doctor?"

Gillian gave a long, weary sigh. Who knew if Owen was better looking? She couldn't judge him objectively. All she knew was that his eyes were dark and bright and bewitching all at once, and that his voice could reach through her skin to caress her soul, and that his touch was hypnotic, rendering her unable to think clearly, unable to know herself or care what happened to her, as long as he kept touching her.

"I can't see him again," she said in a broken, rueful tone. "He makes me crazy."

"You told me today that you knew him in Italy."

"How I know him is irrelevant. The truth is, I don't really know him at all. I was hoping I could spend this evening figuring out what to do about him, but you ruined that for me, Nance. You told him where to find me, and he found me and I couldn't figure out anything."

"I'm sorry," Nancy said genuinely. "Is there any way I can make it better? How about if I take you out to lunch tomorrow?"

"In New York?"

"Sure. Here's an idea—why don't you let me see what I can dig up about him?"

"Don't waste your time." Gillian recalled the thick folder of information about Moore Enterprises sitting on her kitchen table. "I already dug."

"You dug in New Jersey, toots. My information is better. I'm on Wall Street. I can find out who finances him, who processes his money, whether he owns any congressmen and how much he paid in taxes last year. All you can find out is whether he dismembered any labor unions."

"I don't know if I want to find out his financial situation."

"It might make things clearer, Gillian. Maybe my sources will tell me that he's about to be indicted for bribing the SEC, and it'll be easier for you to hate him."

"Hating him should be easy already," Gillian protested. "I'm sure if I put my mind to it, I can learn to hate him without any help from you."

"On the other hand," Nancy went on, "I might find out that he's secretly financing AIDS research and he's breeding endangered species in his backyard. And then you can love him."

"God forbid," Gillian muttered.

"So, what do you say? Lunch tomorrow. Meet me in my office at twelve and I'll give you whatever I've unearthed on your Mr. Moore."

"I don't have my calendar in front of me," Gillian hedged, although she knew she would wind up shuttling into Manhattan for lunch with Nancy. She needed to talk to her friend, face to face, heart to heart. No class-action suit could be as important as that.

"If I don't hear from you, I'll expect you at the stroke of noon."

"Okay."

"You aren't really angry with me, are you?"

Gillian sighed once more. "No, Nancy. I'm angry with myself. But you can still pay for lunch."

With a chuckle, Nancy bade her goodbye.

Gillian returned her telephone to her night table and pushed herself up to sit. The shade trembled against the window, responding to a breeze.

She stood and padded barefoot across the carpet to the window. Lifting the blind, she peeked out.

The unfamiliar car was gone. The block was quiet, tranquil, devoid of mysterious prowlers.

He had looked a little like Owen, hadn't he?

Sure, she thought, letting the blind drop back into place. The stranger she'd spotted down the street resembled Owen Moore about as much as she resembled a cold bronze statue of Juliet in a courtyard seven thousand miles away.

If he looked like Owen, it was only because everybody looked like Owen. Shadows looked like Owen. The moon looked like Owen, the stars, the night.

Her dreams looked like Owen.

And she wasn't going to be able to fall asleep.

Chapter Eight

"Snap out of it, Owen," Ben chided.

"Snap out of what?"

"All morning you've been acting like a zombie. These meetings are important, or we wouldn't be wasting our time."

Owen sighed and stared through the tinted window of the limousine Ben had leased for their day in Manhattan. The car's interior smelled of leather, lemon soap and a faint trace of old cigarette smoke. On the other side of the window, the city bustled; pedestrians hurried along the sidewalks, cabs zipped recklessly through the intersections and buses swerved to and from the curb. It seemed as if everyone had a purpose, a goal, a reason to be traveling from here to there.

Owen had a purpose and a goal, too. He and Ben had already talked with a couple of investment bankers. Now they were on their way to meet an attorney Marc Utrecht had recommended. The firm needed to line up someone licensed to practice locally, in case legal problems cropped up.

Owen understood the necessity of this outing. During his conversations with the investment bankers, he'd clicked into a professional mind-set, raising valid questions, offering insightful arguments, concentrating on the moment.

But as soon as he'd climbed back into the limo, he'd drifted back into the swirling, churning miasma of his private thoughts, his odd memories of the previous evening, his need for something more than the right banker and the right lawyer.

Last night, after he'd driven away from the house where he'd thought he had seen Gillian, he'd cruised back to the main boulevard. Tired of not knowing where he was, he'd pulled into a parking space near the church, hoping that a man of the cloth would offer better directions back to Fort Lee than the bartender had.

A man of the cloth might also tell Owen what the real name of the town was. He simply couldn't believe it was called Verona.

The church looked gloomy from the outside, its dark brownstone facade embellished with leering gargoyles and its spire ominously tall and pointed. No light shone through the narrow stained-glass windows lining the sides of the building.

Owen climbed the steps and pulled on the tarnished brass handle. The thick oak door swung open, and he ventured inside.

The interior of the church smelled of incense. The flame from votive candles in red glasses flickered at a side altar. Ahead of him loomed the main chapel, awash in shadows leaping and dancing from candlelight. The interior was as Gothic and forboding as the outside.

Owen walked slowly down the center aisle. Near the front, he spotted a man kneeling in a pew, his hands clasped before him in prayer. Owen took a seat a few rows behind the man. He didn't want to interrupt the man's prayers just to ask for directions to Fort Lee.

He waited patiently, breathing in the pungent burnt scent of the air and watching the way the hundreds of candles shed tremulous light against the walls and the stained-glass windows. When he closed his eyes he visualized the woman he'd seen silhouetted against her living-room drapes, the woman who had so closely resembled Gillian in his imagination. Then he visualized Gillian herself, at her aunt's house, touching his fingers through the fence.

"Can I help you, son?"

He opened his eyes to discover the man who had been praying now seated in the pew directly in front of him. His white collar and black shirt identified him as a priest; his bald pate and bifocal glasses placed him on the far side of middle age.

"I'm lost," Owen told him.

"Then you've come to the right place."

"No—I mean, I'm trying to get to Fort Lee."

"Ah." The priest mulled over this revelation. "I'm better at spiritual direction than the other kind, but maybe I can help you. Do you know where Pleasant Valley Road is?"

"I don't even know where *I* am."

"Ah." The priest dug a handkerchief from the pocket of his crisp black trousers, then removed his eyeglasses and polished them. "We're back to the spiritual, then."

"No, look—I'm sorry. I'm not even Catholic."

"That's all right. Even non-Catholics need to know where they are."

Owen smiled slightly. "So, where am I?"

"Verona."

"Really?"

"Would I lie?"

Owen took in the man's authoritative white collar and serene countenance and conceded the point with a grin. "I don't suppose you would." His grin faded as he considered his situation. "It's just that... Verona has a special meaning for me. I don't think you'd understand, Mr....?"

"Father Lawrence," the priest introduced himself. "And it's my job to understand. Even if you aren't Catholic. Why does Verona have a special meaning for you?"

"There's a woman—I don't know whether you'd understand that, either, but..." He didn't know why he felt comfortable confiding in Father Lawrence, but the words came easily. "I met a woman in Verona, Italy. Something happened between us."

"You don't have to go into details if you don't want to," the priest assured him.

"There aren't any details to go into. To tell you the truth, I wish there were. But... it's just that ever since I met her, I can't get her out of my mind."

"Are you in love?"

"I can't be in love. I don't even know her."

"Then perhaps you should get to know her."

Owen nodded at the sage, simple advice. "Why am I in Verona, Father Lawrence? Am I ever going to be able to find my way back?"

"Back to where? It may be that you haven't gotten lost. Maybe this is where you belong."

"My home is in southern California. I'm just here in New Jersey on business."

"And you have a woman in Verona, Italy. Perhaps what you need to do, young man, is decide what's the most important thing to you—home, business or love."

The priest gave him directions back to the highway and Owen eventually made his way back to the hotel, where he spent a sleepless night racked by questions.

The same questions continued to haunt him today as he and Ben shuttled around lower Manhattan in the limousine. Who was the woman he'd seen in the house? Why had he driven to Verona? How was he going to get to know Gillian?

What was most important? Home, business or love?

"According to Marc," Ben was saying, "Harvey Shoup is the best."

Shoup? Why did that sound familiar? "The best what?" Owen asked cautiously.

"The best acquisitions attorney in New York. His practice extends across the river, too, so if you have any problems in New Jersey, he can do the troubleshooting for you. I hope you don't have problems with Sandifer, but given the reputation of that maniacal unionist, Sam Chappell, I wouldn't count on smooth sailing."

"What's this lawyer's name, again?"

"Harvey Shoup."

Shoup was not a common name. Owen was certain he'd heard it before, but he didn't know when or in what context. Once again he felt himself being sucked back into the miasma, that trance-like state where everything was an echo of something else: the woman in the house an echo of Gillian, the town an echo of Verona, Italy. Now *Shoup,* an echo of something someone had said to him not long ago.

What did it signify?

When was he going to be sane again?

The limo pulled up to the curb in a no-parking zone in front of an imposing skyscraper. The driver held open the door and Ben told him that they would be out in a half hour or so. Then, his elegant Coach briefcase gripped in his hand and his mile-high forehead glistening with sweat from the late spring heat, he led Owen into the building.

The offices of Shoup, Hawley, Brigham, Weinstein and Associates occupied several upper floors of the building. Owen and Ben stepped out of the elevator into the reception area on the twenty-fifth floor and identified themselves to the receptionist, who lifted her sleek beige telephone and announced them.

After a couple of minutes a young woman opened one of the glass doors separating the reception area from the law offices and beckoned Owen and Ben inside. A few secretarial desks stood in the main room, positioned like sentries guarding the private offices. Ben and Owen followed the secretary along the perimeter of the room, passing one desk, a partitioned photocopy room, a huge potted plant, another desk, an even larger potted plant. Across the room a door opened and a woman emerged.

Gillian.

Oh, man—he was truly crazy. Now he was seeing her everywhere!

As impossible as it was, the woman visible through the fronds of the potted palm looked exactly like Gillian—the lush tumble of tawny hair, the slim, healthy figure clothed in a utilitarian linen suit, the neatly tapering calves, the moss green eyes.

Another woman stepped out of the office, and the woman with the tawny hair and green eyes stepped back in, slamming the door behind her.

Owen froze. He'd seen the other woman before. Her jet black hair and porcelain complexion looked annoyingly familiar. He could almost smell the rose blossoms and hear the chattering British tourists quoting lines of Shakespeare....

The courtyard. In Verona. That was where he'd seen the woman.

She was Gillian's friend.

My name is Nancy Burdette, she had said. *I'm an attorney with Shoup, Hawley in Manhattan. I'm calling for Gillian Chappell.*

"Oh, my God," he whispered.

Ben glanced over his shoulder. "What?"

"I have to talk to that woman." Owen brushed past the foliage and headed across the room to Nancy Burdette.

"Owen—"

He ignored Ben. The black-haired woman in the chic violet silk suit gaped at him as he neared her. "Nancy Burdette," he said when he was close enough for her to hear him.

She continued to gape. He admired her pale skin, her straight nose and her large almond-shaped eyes. She was really quite pretty. Not his type, though. His type was hiding behind the door. "Let me see Gillian."

"You're him, aren't you?"

"I'm Owen Moore. That *is* Gillian in there, isn't it?"

Nancy gave him a slow, calculating perusal. "You're Owen Moore," she murmured with a slight nod.

"I'd like to see Gillian. May I go in?"

"You didn't come here to see her, did you? No," she answered herself, "you couldn't have. Me? You wanted to see me? My secretary—"

"I came to see Harvey Shoup. But if Gillian's in there, I'd rather see her."

"I don't know. We're about to leave for lunch." Nancy appraised him with another sweeping glance.

"I'm in enough hot water with Gillian for telling you where her aunt lived. If she wants to hide in my office until you fall off the face of the earth, I'll let her."

"I'm not going to fall off the face of the earth," he warned. "I'm going to stand here until I see her."

Nancy eyed him a moment longer. "You know, you're causing me a lot of trouble," she muttered, reaching across her secretary's desk for the telephone. "If Gillian doesn't want to see you, I'll guard this door with my life. Do you understand? I blew it yesterday and I'm not going to blow it today. Gillian's friendship is too important to me."

Owen was about to issue some reassurances, but before he could speak she had pressed two buttons on the phone console. Through the closed office door, Owen heard the muffled sound of a phone chirping.

"Gillian? It's me," Nancy said into the phone.

Owen wanted to press his ear to the door and hear what Gillian had to say. That would be too obvious, however, so he restrained himself and listened to Nancy's end of the conversation.

"He says he has an appointment with Harvey. It's pure coincidence," Nancy said, sending Owen a suspicious glance. "Or so he says."

His patience, threadbare to begin with, disintegrated completely. He reached across the desk and swiped the receiver out of Nancy's hands. "Gillian," he said, clinging to the receiver as if it were a lifeline. "Please let me in."

"Have you followed me here?" she asked, her tone deceptively even. "You followed me last night, and now this. There are stalker laws, Owen."

"I'm not stalking you, Gillian. You know that."

"Okay, you're not stalking me. How did you find me here today? Did some voice in the oven direct you?"

"You heard Nancy. I've got a meeting with Harvey Shoup. I didn't know you'd be here. I didn't even know Nancy would be here." When she didn't respond, he murmured, "Let me in, Gillian. Open the door."

He heard a click as she hung up the phone and his heart plummeted, weighted down with sadness and disappointment. He'd been sure Gillian had more guts than to hide from him so cravenly.

Then he heard another click, coming from the direction of the door. The click of a lock being undone. The door swung inward a couple of inches. Gillian remained invisible inside.

Before Nancy could interfere, Owen darted around the desk, slipped into the office and locked the door behind himself.

Gillian stood near a wall lined with oak bookshelves, filled with uniformly bound law books. The office was small but neat, with a tidy oak desk, a small window and a framed photo of Nancy mugging in front of the statue of Juliet.

He remembered Gillian snapping that photo.

His attention shifted from the statue to Gillian, looking somewhat grim but utterly beautiful in her plain gray suit, with her face devoid of cosmetics and her feet shoved into boring flat-heeled pumps. Her hair, at least, wasn't plain. It fell in a jumble of gold-tinged waves past her shoulders, reminding him of yesterday's summer rain, of the clouds drifting across the moon, of the crickets, of the brush of her fingertips against his through the fence.

Her green eyes remained fixed on him. If she'd hoped to look impassive she failed; despite her grim expression, her eyes were alive with turbulent emotion.

"I don't know about you," he said, smiling sheepishly, "but I'm slowly going insane. Maybe not so slowly. If we don't work this thing out I'm going to be spending the rest of my life in a discreet institution somewhere, bouncing off the padded walls."

In spite of herself she laughed. "You don't look that far gone to me."

"I put up a good front."

She lowered her eyes. Released from their mesmerizing beauty, he shifted his gaze downward, to the graceful line of her jaw, her throat, her hands. He wanted those hands on him, those arms around him. He wanted her mouth on his.

He saw two options: kiss her that instant, or sign himself into the discreet institution with the padded walls.

He crossed the small office to her. Rather than pressing back into the bookshelves, she held her ground, lifted her chin and awaited his offensive without flinching. When he reached ground zero, the toes of his loafers a half inch from the toes of her pumps, she refused to shrink from him. When he lifted his hands to her soft peach-hued cheeks, she didn't turn away. When he lowered his lips to hers, she sighed, closed her eyes and met him, if not eagerly, at least willingly.

Several minutes later he came up for air. At the first contact every muscle in his body had strung itself taut, but then he'd relaxed into the kiss and let the heat melt inside him rather than galvanize him. He'd felt no less aroused, but it had been an easy, friendly arousal, something he could enjoy without losing his control over.

Pulling back from her at last, he was pleased to see that she looked only slightly flustered. Her eyes remained clear, her cheeks flushed with pleasure, her breath deep and unnaturally even. He watched the rhythmic rise and fall of her breasts under her clothing, the play of her tongue over her lips, the flutter in her neck as she swallowed.

For a long moment, the only sound in the room was the sibilant whisper of the air conditioner. Then Gillian spoke. "We hardly know each other."

"I'm aware of that."

"We can't keep meeting like this." She grinned apologetically at the cliché.

"How should we meet?"

Again her tongue darted out and flicked over her lips. He followed the motions of the tiny pink tip and imagined her tongue in his mouth, on his chest, licking downward.... The sensation that bolted through him wasn't an easy, familiar arousal. It was arousal, all right—fierce and demanding.

"Could we maybe go out for a drink?"

"Now?" He would reschedule his appointment with Harvey Shoup. Or else Ben could take care of it while Owen ran off with Gillian. Nothing, not even securing a strong legal representative on the East Coast, was as essential as making sense of his relationship with Gillian, making a success of it.

"This evening," she said.

"Fine."

"It'll have to be late—say, eight o'clock? I've got tons of work to catch up on."

He nodded. "Eight o'clock is fine. Can I pick you up at your house?"

"All right—but we're going out, Owen. I want that clear. We aren't going to stay in."

"I understand."

"I mean it," she insisted, evidently not quite trusting him. "We have to get to know each other better. We have to talk."

"Okay." As much as he wanted to get to know her in the most basic biblical sense, he respected the wisdom of her demand. There was always a chance that if he got a closer look at Gillian's mind, at her personality, her likes and dislikes and tastes and habits, he might find her less appealing. He owed himself the chance to regain his sanity by falling out of love with her before he surrendered to the possibility that he was in love with her.

"Let me jot down my address," she said, moving toward Nancy's desk in a wide arc so she wouldn't accidentally brush against Owen. She pulled out a piece of notepaper and a pen from the Lucite desk set and wrote her address and phone number. Then she handed him the piece of paper.

The word *Verona* leaped out at him.

He covered his reflexive gasp with a long breath. It *did* say Verona. Rose Lane, in Verona, New Jersey.

"It isn't hard to get to," she told him. "You take the Pleasant Valley exit off 280...."

Cripes. She lived in Verona.

He'd been on her street last night. It was Gillian he'd seen through the window. Gillian, who must have left the family barbecue—and the blond hunk—right after Owen had left the playground, and driven home, and gazed out her living-room window as he'd gazed in.

Gillian, who lived only a few blocks from the church where Owen had asked Father Lawrence to help him find his way back to where he belonged.

He'd been exactly where he'd belonged, all along.

"I'll find it," he assured her. He'd heard so many recitations of 280 and I-95 and Pleasant Valley last night. He'd driven on the roads, off the roads, in and out of Verona until it had seemed less like a town than Alice's Wonderland or Dorothy's Oz, a mystifying magical place which one could leave only after panicking and paying one's dues and trusting oneself.

He folded the paper and tucked it into an inner pocket of his jacket, close to his heart.

"I'll find it," he said again, a promise, a vow, an acknowledgment that his entire future—his very existence—depended on having the courage to return to Verona.

Chapter Nine

"He is lost," Juliet lamented. "He has already driven to her village, to her cottage—and yet less than twenty-four hours later he cannot seem to find his way back to the place where he has been."

"Ah, 'tis true." Romeo issued a melodramatic sigh. "How will he find his beloved Gillian tonight? Last night, he found her without looking for her."

"He was looking for her last night," Juliet argued. "He has been looking for her for two years, dear Romeo. Perhaps he did not realize it, but he has been looking for his Gillian ever since he touched my statue."

"Ever since you began your good-hearted meddling."

Juliet parried Romeo's gentle gibe with one of her own. "He should stop and ask for directions, but alas, he will not. He is a man, and men are incapable of making so simple an inquiry."

"He asked for directions last night, and those directions rendered him more deeply lost than when he'd started his journey," Romeo argued. "Besides, there is nothing simple in revealing to the world one's ignorance. On my way to Mantua, I too grew confused as to my whereabouts. Yet I found my destination without *resorting to the humiliation of imploring strangers to direct me.''*

"*And having found Mantua, you should have stayed there,*" Juliet chided. "*Had you but stayed in Mantua instead of returning to Verona and discovering me in my death trance, our story might have ended differently.*"

"*Our story has ended, in any case,*" Romeo reminded her. "*But what of the story of this troubled pair, Owen Moore and Gillian Chappell? He drives madly hither and yon in search of a strange Verona in a place not at all like our beautiful Italy. And she sits at home brooding over the course upon which she has embarked. What shall she do if he does not appear at her door soon? She may resent him, or think him a knave for making her wait.*"

Juliet agreed. She herself was beginning to resent Owen's refusal to stop at the church, which he had driven past not once but twice, and bid the good Father Lawrence help him. "*If he desires Gillian enough, he should swallow his pride and ask for directions,*" she observed primly.

"*Surely he desires her, very much,*" Romeo observed. "*As someone who was once a mere man, I know that desire very well. It is a hunger that can compel a man to swallow anything, even pride.*"

"*Hunger! I thought we were discussing love.*"

"*To a man, love and hunger overlap—and to a woman, as well. You need not act so affronted, my bride. The hunger of which we speak reflected your appetite as well as mine, even though you were then an untouched maiden. And your Owen and Gillian are ravenously hungry for each other now. Look at her, waiting for him.*"

Juliet observed how Gillian fretted, how she wrung her hands and fussed with her image in the looking glass and spoke into the air, issuing strange mumbles that expressed naught so much as her doubt about the path she had chosen. Ravenous was not a term Juliet would use to describe Gillian's mood, but the woman was clearly tormented by needs and wants—and anxiety about their propriety.

"Were you afraid that night, awaiting me?" Romeo asked.

She knew what night he was speaking of, the night she became his mate not just in the eyes of God but in her soul and her flesh. She had awaited him not with fear but with the joy of knowing that her body would soon shed its immature youth and embrace womanhood, that she would be a wife in the arms of her beloved Romeo. "I should have been afraid," she admitted. "You had just slain my dear cousin—"

"Because he had slain my dear friend."

"I do not need your justification, Romeo. I accept what happened as an inexorable step toward our tragic end. Yet still I received you into my bed that night. Perhaps I should have felt some hesitancy, but I was too young to understand the sorrow that can befall a woman in love."

"Gillian understands," Romeo guessed, watching the woman as she moved to her looking glass once more and ran a brush through her luxuriant golden brown tresses. "She is older than you were then, and perhaps wiser. Wise enough to be afraid."

"Afraid, yet brave," Juliet said. "Like me, she knows that there can be no love without risk—and she is brave enough to take that risk."

"So you hope."

"So I pray, Romeo. So I pray."

EIGHT-THIRTY, AND NO SIGN of Owen.

Maybe he'd come to his senses. If he had, she ought to be celebrating, not pacing around her house, eating herself up with doubt.

It was all right. They would talk tonight—if Owen ever showed up. They would talk, and she would find out how much of the incriminating record Nancy had compiled about Moore Enterprises was true, how much was Owen's father's doing and how much was Owen's. She would try to maintain an open mind, even though page after page of the files Nancy had handed her over lunch that day had described the firm's cutthroat treatment of the people who worked for its acquisitions.

One union had filed a complaint against Moore Enterprises with the National Labor Relations Board. Within a week, the leader of the union local had been stopped by the police on his way home from an organizational meeting and a plastic bag containing a mysterious white powder had been found in his glove compartment. He'd sworn it had been planted, but by the time the case was thrown out of court he'd lost the union's backing. His replacement had been ineffectual, a pawn of management. Within a year, the workers had had a pay cut forced upon them, under threat of losing their jobs altogether.

Gillian wondered whether her father might someday soon be stopped and searched, whether some corrupt cop might find a bag of powder in his glove compartment.

She would speak to Owen tonight. She would confront him. She would find out what he'd had to do with the sleazy policies outlined in the files Nancy had gathered for her. If Gillian wasn't satisfied by his answers, she'd fight him with everything she had—her brain, her law degree and her passion.

And if she *was* satisfied . . . A memory of his sweet, sensual kiss filled her. A memory of his inability to keep his distance in Nancy's office, of her inability to fend him off—her deliberate decision to accept what he needed to give her at that moment.

Of course, the entire matter might never come up, if he didn't show his face soon.

She returned to her bedroom one final time and appraised her reflection in the mirror above her dresser. There was nothing suggestive in her outfit—a lacy white sweater, a flaring floral-print skirt that fell nearly to her ankles, and white leather sandals. She'd brushed her hair into a loose cascade of waves, glossed her lips with a soft peach hue and added a whisper of blush to her cheeks. She looked modest, feminine . . . and remarkably plain.

Why her? She wasn't insecure, but she was a realist and—other than the stupid myth of the Juliet statue— she could think of no good reason Owen would have chosen her as the object of his desire. The world was filled with prettier women, sexier women, women whose politics and professional aims would make a better fit with his.

Maybe he was after her as a way to get to her father, and through him, the union. Maybe Owen thought that if he romanced her, she would keep her father from crossing swords with him.

If he thought that, he was as wrong as could be.

With a sigh, she turned off the bedroom light and returned to the living room. Pulling back the drape, she gazed out through the window at the darkening sky, seeking answers in the first of the night's stars.

So it was well past the time she'd expected him to arrive. So she wasn't a gorgeous, glamorous femme fatale. Despite all that, Gillian knew in her heart that Owen was on his way to Verona, to her.

"Come, night! come, Owen..."

The words seemed to rise from a dimly lit corner of her mind. It was a line from Shakespeare, part of some soliloquy she'd had to memorize ages ago for a high-school English class.

Wait a minute. She'd never read a Shakespearean play with a character named Owen in it!

Yet the words continued to surface, bubbling up from a well of long dormant memories and spilling into the air. *"For thou wilt lie upon the wings of night..."*

Romeo and Juliet. She remembered where the speech came from: the scene in which Juliet had stood in her house, impatient for the night to come and bring her lover to her. Juliet had said, "Come, Romeo," but "Come, Owen" sounded right to Gillian.

She continued to gaze through the living-room window, watching as, one after another, the stars winked to silver life in the clear, dark sky. *"Come, gentle night; come, loving black-brow'd night, Give me my Owen..."*

Juliet had recited her speech after she and Romeo had been secretly married. Gillian ran the scene through her head. With a slight start, she realized that in the scene Juliet was eagerly awaiting Romeo's arrival so they could consummate their marriage.

"Well," she said with as much certainty as she could muster, "Owen and I aren't going to consummate anything."

But Shakespeare's poetry continued to sing inside her, echoing Juliet's plea. *If love be blind, it best agrees with night. Come, civil night... all in black, and learn me how to lose a winning match..."*

"I'm not going to lose anything," Gillian snapped, letting the curtain drop back into place against the windowsill. "Owen isn't coming. It's too late. If he were going to come, he'd be here by now."

The doorbell rang.

She felt her pulse leap, race, flitter wildly through her body. Her breath caught in her throat; her fingers grew icy.

He was here. If he wasn't, if someone else was standing on her front porch...then she would know for sure that Owen was never going to come.

But she knew for sure that he *was* going to come, that he already had come, that he was just a few steps away, separated from her by nothing more than her front door. He had flown to her on the wings of night, and now, in the starlit darkness, he was here.

This wasn't a match, she consoled herself, taking deep breaths and ordering her nervous system to calm down. Nobody was going to win or lose. She and Owen were going to say hello and go out for a drink. She was going to ask him what his intentions were regarding Sandifer Chemicals. She was going to be her father's advocate, not a woman Owen could march across a room and kiss without having to overcome even an ounce of resistance on her part.

She swept her hands through her hair, straightened her sweater and arranged her lips into a cordial smile. Squaring her shoulders, she walked briskly to the front door and opened it.

Owen stood on the porch, holding a single red rose. She tried to focus on the flower, but her gaze was drawn irresistibly to his face, his eyes hidden in shadow, his black hair tossed by the wind. He smelled of mint and freshly mown grass and clean, potent masculinity.

She couldn't say hello. Couldn't say anything. All she could do was stare at him.

He extended the rose and she managed to take it. Then he stepped into the house and closed the door behind him.

Her fingers fisted around the rigid stem of the flower. She lowered her eyes from Owen's face to the flower's delicate red bud, noting en route the loose fit of his blazer, the crisp cotton of his shirt, the relaxed fall of his trousers, his hand-stitched loafers. Slowly she raised her head again, absorbing the reality of him in her house, electrifying the air, permeating the atmosphere with his presence.

"Gillian."

That was all. Just her name, spoken in a low, husky sigh. And then his arms were around her and his mouth was taking hers.

She was vaguely aware of him lifting her, cradling her against his strong, firm chest. Her tongue battled his; her breath merged with his. Her hand at the back of his head clutched the rose, as if holding it was the only thing that kept her from disintegrating.

Kissing him felt too good, too honest, too necessary. She tried to hang onto her misgivings, the ugly things she'd read about his company and his father. She tried to hang onto the idea of going somewhere with him to talk. But her ability to think evaporated in the consuming heat of his embrace, his mouth welded to hers, his heart pounding against her breast.

Without breaking the kiss, he carried her down the short hallway to her bedroom. When he reached the side of her bed he lowered her to her feet. His mouth remained on hers, nibbling, teasing and then overpowering her with passionate intensity.

I hardly know him, she thought. *What I know frightens me.*

But his kiss told her everything she needed to know—his kiss and his warmth and his large deft hands cupping her shoulders and gliding down her arms, spanning her waist and releasing the button of her skirt.

She felt the garment slide along her bare legs and pool around her ankles. She ought to have protested, reared back and slapped his face—yet she wanted this, needed it as much as he did. There would be time later to assess the damage, time later to chastise herself for her recklessness. Time later to think about how wrong this was.

At that moment, it was right.

She wedged her fingers under the collar of his jacket and pushed it off his shoulders, down his arms. He let it fall to the floor, then brought his hands to her sweater and undid the buttons, one and then the next and the next, until the delicately crocheted material parted. With a barely audible groan, he lowered his lips to the rounded flesh above the lace trim of her brassiere.

Her legs felt weak, and she sank down onto the mattress. Owen reached behind her for the clasp of her bra; she reached forward for the buckle of his belt. Her bra fell loose the instant the belt came undone. Owen's fingers flexed against the silky skin of her back as she unfastened his fly.

With obvious reluctance, he drew back from her, pulling off her sweater and bra and tossing them aside.

She shifted onto her knees so she could get at his shirt while he shed his trousers. Her fingers trembled, but he refused to assist her. He simply observed as she fumbled with the buttons, until at last they were all open.

His chest was glorious. Perfect. A smooth bronze expanse of streamlined muscle and sinew tapering down to a taut, flat abdomen. She ran her hands over his skin, traced his ribs through the athletically lean flesh, rose to his nipples and watched as they hardened into points.

Her own nipples hardened in empathy.

She felt his heartbeat against her palm, felt the raggedness of his breath. She let her hands glide as high as his collarbone and then brought them down again, following the sleek male contours of his torso, the arch of his rib cage, the surface of his stomach. When she reached the edge of his briefs she paused.

He covered her hands with his, curled her fingers around the elastic waistband and pushed against her knuckles, guiding her as she removed the last of his clothing. Her fingertips brushed through the thick, dark hair at his groin and he groaned again, a low, helpless sound in the shadowed room.

He brought one of her hands to him, pressing his hot, swollen flesh into the hollow of her palm. This time the groan came from her.

The room seemed to whirl—and then she realized it was Owen turning her, pressing her down against the pillows and sprawling alongside her. Propped up on one arm, he lowered his mouth to hers as his free hand stripped away her panties, plucked off her sandals and roamed the length of her legs. His kisses were deep, wet, greedy. His hand was magic, dancing across her skin, discovering the dimples at the backs of her knees, playing over the angles of her hip bones, fondling her navel and then rising higher to circle one breast and then the other.

She arched her back, needing more, more of his touch, more of his love. He cupped one breast, squeezed it, massaged it until she could scarcely breathe from the excruciating pleasure. When he tore his mouth from hers, she moaned in protest—until he brought his lips to her breast and her moan dissolved into a sigh of ecstasy.

His hands continued to move, one on her other breast and one traveling from her waist to the outer surface of her thigh, caressing, kneading, coaxing her legs apart. Her hands journeyed over him as well, stretching to reach as much of his back as she could, exploring the strong ridges of his shoulders, twining through the soft black waves of his hair.

When he lifted his mouth she slid her fingers forward to his chest. He rose higher, and she pulled herself against him and grazed her lips along his shoulder. She nipped gently at his skin with her teeth, then flicked her tongue across it. He tasted hot, smooth, salty. Intoxicating.

His hand stirred once more, rounding her thigh and rising to the nest of hair between her legs. With a sharp, searing glide he entered her, claimed her with his fingers, probed and pressed and filled her with sensations too sweet to bear.

She fell back, gasping, shaking her head. She was too close, too ready. She needed him with her or she would die.

Gathering what little strength she had left, she nudged his hand away, grasped his hips and pulled him down to her. He braced himself above her and thrust deep, filling her, igniting her.

Her body throbbed, surged and ebbed around him, released itself again and again in a dark, devastating cadence. She struggled to keep breathing, moving, bringing him pleasure. She was embarrassed by how quickly she'd peaked, but when she dared to open her eyes she found Owen smiling above her, taking delight in her satisfaction even though he hadn't achieved his own.

He withdrew and thrust again, fierce, hard plunges that refused her a chance to recover. She ringed her legs around him, wanting to give him as much as he'd given her, wanting to give him more.

He gave her more, as well. His body stroked hers, heated it, generated new sensations, new tensions, deep, billowing bursts of ecstasy. He wedged one hand under her hips, angling her to increase the contact between their bodies. His other hand he tangled deep into her hair, holding her head steady as his mouth came down on hers.

The world shattered. The earth spun away. There was nothing but energy, an explosion of bliss shooting through her in heavenly pulses, shooting through Owen, uniting them into a single fiery essence, two souls wedded into one.

An eternity passed before she came back to herself, before she became conscious of the rumpled summer quilt beneath her and the spread of moonlight blanketing her body and Owen's. He lay on top of her, heavy and damp with sweat, his lips buried in her hair and his hand strumming lazily across her shoulder. Feeling him soften and slide from her, she tightened her arms around him, needing his nearness even more. When she sensed him pulling back, she let out a quiet moan. "Don't go."

"I won't." He eased off her and rolled onto his side, then guided her onto her side so she was facing him. His motions were sluggish and sweet as he adjusted the pillow beneath her head and lifted a heavy mussed lock of her hair back from her face.

She gazed at him, at his fine, strong features, his eyes glowing enigmatically, his smile inscrutable. She savored the warmth of his hand gliding down to the small of her back, his insteps rubbing the soles of her feet, his chest moving against hers as he labored to breathe normally. His free hand captured hers and held it between them, his thumb meandering along the tips of her fingers.

She studied the hand that embraced hers, the thickness of his fingers entwined with hers. "I'm not like this," she murmured, reliving her astonishing response to him and experiencing a fresh rush of embarrassment.

"Like what?"

"I don't make love with strangers."

"I'm not a stranger."

Gathering her courage, she forced her gaze back to his face. He *was* a stranger—yet she knew his eyes, knew their dark beauty, their constancy, the profound devotion they reflected. The information her own research and Nancy's had unearthed about Moore Enterprises might have revealed certain facts about Owen, but what she'd just experienced with him—what she had *always* experienced with him—had less to do with facts than with truth.

This was the truth: she loved him. Whoever he was, whatever he had done, whatever he would do in the future, she loved him.

If love be blind, it best agrees with night, Juliet had said as she'd awaited her Romeo. In the night, in the unlit intimacy of her bed, Gillian was willing to acknowledge that her love for Owen was blind. That didn't make it any less real or powerful.

The thought brought her little comfort. Accepting that she was in love with the man who ran a company with a reputation for ruining innocent people's lives filled her with apprehension.

He must have seen the dismay in her expression. He drew her hand to his lips and kissed her palm. "Tell me," he said.

"It's nothing."

"It's something. Don't lie. I need your honesty, Gillian."

She took a deep breath and let it out. "It's just . . . I know we touched the statue and nothing else is supposed to matter, but . . . but it *does* matter, Owen. It *does*."

"What matters?"

"Who you are. What you do."

He touched her knuckles with his lips once more, then let their hands come to rest, cushioned against her breasts. "Who I am is Owen Moore. What I do is drive all over northern New Jersey looking for some obscure road named Rose Lane in a town called Verona. What I do is spend the past two years of my life dreaming about a beautiful, elusive woman. And then I find her in a cozy little house, waiting for me, and I'm the happiest man in the world."

The sheer romance in his words momentarily silenced her. Lord help her, she wanted to remain blind. She didn't want to turn a bright light on the truth and discover it was only facts, a heap of hard, nasty facts about the ruthlessness of the Moore family.

But she couldn't wish herself blind. She had to open her eyes. "I was referring to what you do profession-ally."

"Professionally? Who I am is the president of Moore Enterprises. What I do is finance acquisitions."

"Who you are," she said quietly, "is the son of Franklin Moore. And what you do is buy companies and destroy the people who work for them."

Her accusation took him aback. He studied her war-ily, then exhaled. "This is what I get for demanding honesty."

"I'm afraid so."

He shook his head and gave her hand a squeeze. "I'm myself, Gillian, not my father. I don't destroy people."

She bit her lip, forcing herself to forget the sublime lovemaking they'd shared just minutes ago and con-centrate on the present, his claims, this miserable talk they had to have. They should have had it somewhere else, with their clothes on and a table between them, but it was too late for should-haves.

"You've asked me to be honest, and I am being hon-est," she said, her voice wavering. "But you're lying to me."

His eyes grew cold, stony. "Who do you think I've destroyed?"

"The people who worked for Great Western Air-lines. The people who worked for Hardy Electronics. The people who worked—"

"Stop." His hand tightened painfully around hers, but that was nothing compared to the agony inside her, the desperate pain squeezing her heart.

She forced herself to continue. If she and Owen were headed for disaster she wanted to get it over with right away, before she could grow accustomed to loving him. "Moore Enterprises bought those outfits and decimated them. I didn't want to believe it, Owen, but I've done some research about your company. I've read up on your methods. I know how you treat anyone who challenges your authority in a new acquisition."

"You don't know anything." Although soft, his voice held a very real menace.

Hers, on the other hand, sounded anguished. "Then tell me, Owen. Tell me how you justify the way you devastated those companies for a profit. Tell me why Hardy Electronics no longer has a plant operating in the United States. Tell me why Great Western no longer exists—and why Moore Enterprises wound up pocketing millions of dollars along the way. Tell me about Art Wilson and the white powder a cop found in his car. Tell me how you can live with yourself, knowing what you've done to these people."

He swore under his breath and rolled away.

She wanted him to convince her she was wrong. She wanted that more than she'd ever wanted anything before. Yet he wasn't even trying to plead his case. He wasn't offering any explanations, any excuses or rationalizations. Other than that one ugly curse, he wasn't saying anything at all.

"Do you deny you did those things?"

He closed his eyes and sighed. A long, tense minute elapsed before he said, "Yes. I deny I did those things."

He was lying. She could tell by his reluctance to answer, by his inability to look at her, to meet her gaze, to take her hand in his again. She had exposed him, challenged him with the truth—and he had lied.

Whatever miracle had occurred between them just moments ago could exist only in the blindness of night. The bright glare of reality annihilated it.

Her eyes stung with tears. She wanted to scream. She wanted to make him hurt as much as she was hurting. She wanted to shake him until his teeth rattled, until his head snapped and his heart broke the way hers was breaking.

"It's wrong," she said, unable to suppress the tremor in her voice. "What you did to those workers was wrong."

"My father bought Great Western Airlines," he said in a low, lifeless tone. "Not me. My father."

"But you were with Moore Enterprises then. You were an executive with the firm. You participated in all the major decisions."

"Yes. I participated in the decision to acquire Great Western. And I advised my father not to touch the union. I fought him with everything I had." The indignation in his voice was mixed with weariness. "I fought him and I lost."

"So you went along with it."

"No. I didn't go along with it. I quit my job. I left Moore Enterprises."

Nancy's data hadn't said anything about Owen's quitting. According to the archives, he had officially joined the firm the day after he'd graduated from Stanford's business school. He was with the firm today. Nothing in the files had mentioned that he'd quit.

"When did you leave?" she asked dubiously.

He shot her a quick, combative look, then turned his attention back to the ceiling. "I don't like this, Gillian. I don't like having to prove myself to you."

She didn't like it, either. But they'd done everything wrong, out of order. If they'd talked before they'd made love, if she'd gotten to know him first...

"When did you leave?" she repeated in a stronger voice.

"Ten months before I met you." His tone was dry, resigned and bitter. "I left California and moved to Italy."

That hadn't come up in the records—but she knew he'd been in Italy. He was telling the truth about that; maybe he was telling the truth about everything.

He'd fought his father. He'd tried to do the right thing and he'd lost. Lost so badly he'd had to leave the country.

Her accusations hung between them, tattered by his angry self-defense and her remorse. Surely he couldn't fault her for having figured he'd been a part of his father's malicious business dealings. She'd been in the dark. She'd made reasonable assumptions. He couldn't blame her.

But he did.

She wondered if he would ever forgive her. If he didn't, she would never forgive herself.

She rose up on one arm and peered down into his face. His eyes were bleak, his mouth set in a grim line, his jaw flexing as he ground his teeth together.

She cupped her hand under his chin and urged him to look at her. "I'm sorry," she whispered.

"Yeah."

"I shouldn't have assumed the worst."

A mirthless smile curved his lip. He covered her hand with his and eased it away from his face. "I'm no fan of my father's business tactics, either. Let's just forget it."

"We can't forget it," she argued. "I said these things—"

"And maybe you hit close to the mark. Okay? I didn't agree with my father, but you had no way of knowing that."

She could see him thawing, the hint of light in his profoundly dark eyes, the relenting of his jaw, the deepening of his breath. The soothing warmth of his hand covering hers.

He guided her hand down to his chest and held it against his heart. His eyes remained on her face, steady, penetrating. His smile faded and when he spoke he sounded solemn, his voice an intense whisper. "Don't judge me, Gillian. I am who I am. That should be enough for you."

She hoped it *would* be enough—because he clearly couldn't promise her more. "I want to believe you, Owen. I want to believe you would never do anything to harm the workers you deal with."

"Like your father?"

"Him and everybody at Sandifer Chemicals. And everybody in every other company Moore gobbles up. They're human beings, Owen. Not just numbers on a balance sheet. They're real people with real lives."

"I'm a real person with a real life, too. I don't go around gobbling up companies and harming employees." He scrutinized her for a moment, then sighed and let his hand fall. "If you can't trust me..."

"I do." The words emerged on their own, a simple, heartfelt expression of faith. "I trust you, Owen." No matter what her mind told her, in her heart she knew that Owen was decent and honorable and good. "I think..." She faltered, afraid of trusting too much, trusting too blindly.

"You think what?"

"I think I'm in love with you."

There. She'd said it. She'd said too many other things already, but this was the most important thing. If he knew that, he might forgive the rest.

The smile that captured his lips took her breath away. "In spite of who I am?"

"In spite of who you are—or because of who you are. Either way."

"Do you wish it were different between us?"

She tentatively returned his smile. "I don't think I have a choice."

"The statue decided for us, didn't it?"

For *us*. He was in love with her, too.

"Yes," she said, accepting the inexplicable, indisputable truth. "The statue decided for us."

She bowed to kiss him.

Chapter Ten

Driving to Verona, he had promised himself that once
he got to Gillian's house he would hand her the rose and
then head out with her to some well-lit public place. He
knew as well as she did what would happen if they
stayed at her house. Cripes, he couldn't even be alone
with her in her friend's office without needing her,
needing to touch her and kiss her and absorb her into
himself.

He'd had plenty of time to plan his evening with her,
given how lost he'd gotten along the way. There was
something about Verona that threw him off. He prided
himself on his ability to get where he was going. But
Verona worked like a magnet on his inner compass,
causing the needle to spin deliriously, pointing every
way and no way.

Maybe the problem was not Verona but Gillian.

He had tried not to become frustrated, but as he'd
driven in one circle and then another, as he'd back-
tracked and detoured and found himself cruising past
Father Lawrence's church for the third time, impatience burgeoned inside him.

He'd had to find Rose Lane. What little sanity he had
left depended on it.

At long last he'd reached Gillian's street. He'd recognized the modest shingled ranch house on the neatly tended quarter-acre plot. It had been the most welcome sight in the world—until she opened her door. Then *she'd* been the most welcome sight.

Give her the flower and get the hell out of the house, he'd ordered himself.

He'd given her the flower and spoken her name.

And then all the frustrations, all the desperate yearning, the fear that he would never find his way back to her, the undefined longing he'd lived with for the past two years, the strange lack in his existence, the aching emptiness that only one particular woman in the universe could fill . . .

That one particular woman had stood in front of him, within his reach. And he'd taken her.

It had happened too fast; it had been too intense. He wanted to love her again, slowly this time. He wanted to taste every inch of her, to learn her every reflex, every response. He wanted to stay inside her forever.

But before he could even catch his breath, she'd started asking questions. Questions that made him wonder whether their spectacular passion was all that held them together.

Did she really doubt him? Did she actually think he was capable of the things she'd accused him of?

Did she think he was like his father?

If she did, could he blame her?

Her lips brushed over his, as soft as velvet, as sweet as honey. He wound his fingers deep into her hair and held her still as he returned her kiss. His body reacted predictably, but his mind held back.

She loved him, but her love was unreasoned. He wanted her to love him consciously, intentionally, willingly.

He had questions, too, questions about the kind of father she had, a father as thirsty for power as his own father. A father who—according to the various documents Harvey Shoup had faxed to the hotel late that afternoon—would do just about anything to triumph over his foe. A father who had contributed to layoffs even more than Franklin Moore had, because Sam Chappell had refused to hold the line on wages or renegotiate contracts when his company was in financial straits. A father who resorted to rabble-rousing when he had no rational basis for his demands, who threatened to shut down businesses with his might, just as Owen's father shut down businesses with his money. A father who had even fought his own union's national officers when they refused to bend to his will.

How much did Gillian have to do with her father's militant union strategies? How well did she use her legal training to prop him up and bail him out?

Owen had questions and concerns, too.

Breaking the kiss, he sank into the pillow, then guided her head to his shoulder and cuddled her against him. He raked his fingers through the long, silky waves of her hair, listened to her breathing, savored the weight of her leg looped over his.

"I want to know more about you," she said, sketching a meandering line across his chest with her index finger. "Tell me everything."

He laughed. "Everything?"

"Start wherever you want."

He coiled a lock of her hair around his thumb and considered his reply. "Everything started when I met you," he said.

She fell silent, and he wondered whether he should have admitted such a thing. It was the truth. He wasn't the sort who could announce to the world that he was in love, so he used the words he felt safe with to express a dangerous reality: he was as much in love with Gillian as she was with him.

She continued to move her finger on him, light and teasing. "What did you do after I left Verona?"

"I left, too. I went back to America."

"Why?"

"Because that's where you were."

"You couldn't have expected to find me. America's a big place."

He shrugged. He plowed his fingers into her hair again, relishing its cool texture, its maverick waves. "It wasn't a conscious decision on my part," he explained. "I had no reason to assume I'd ever see you again, and I don't think that was what I was counting on when I came home. But . . . you left and then I left. It seemed like the only thing to do."

"Did you resume your position at Moore Enterprises then?"

"I didn't go back to the company until about a year ago. I wound up settling in Venice."

He felt her flinch in surprise. "Venice?"

"California. Just south of Los Angeles." He smiled wistfully. "You don't know how close I came to following you to Venice, Italy. But by the time I could have packed up my life and traveled there, I knew you would have been long gone. So I went to Venice, California, instead."

"And I came to Verona, New Jersey."

"Blame it on the statue," he joked, although it really wasn't funny. Like falling for Gillian, his decision to buy a house in Venice had seemed preordained. "I got involved in financing some local entrepreneurs there, people with good ideas and no money. I put together backing, supplied some business counseling, signed on as a silent partner. Those investments are still paying off—and no, I didn't fire anyone."

"If you were doing so well on your own, why did you return to Moore Enterprises?"

"My father had a stroke," he told her.

"I'm sorry, Owen. I didn't know."

Closing his eyes for a minute, he pictured his father in his wheelchair, his left eyelid drooping and the left corner of his mouth permanently skewed. Franklin Moore looked old and frail. If Gillian saw him, she'd be hard pressed to find anything hateful or menacing about him.

Owen remembered the morning a year ago when his father had been far weaker and more lopsided. Owen had been sitting by his father's side at the hospital. A nurse had appeared in the doorway to remind Owen's father that he had a round of physical therapy scheduled and Owen's father had grunted at her to shut up. "I've got to have a word with my boy, first."

My boy. Owen had bristled at the phrase. He was a man, not a boy—and he was his own person, not his father's.

"You'll take over the company," his father had said in his thick, sluggish mumble.

"Let Mom run it."

"She doesn't want to. She wants to stay active, but she doesn't want to have to devote herself completely to it. Running the firm is a full-time commitment."

"Mr. Moore," the nurse had interjected. "The physical therapists are waiting."

"Let 'em wait," he snarled. "Owen, you can do it full-time. You'll have Ben and Marc there, and your mother when she feels like showing up. But you've got the time—and the smarts. You have to take over."

"I can't run it the way you've run it."

"I can't run it at all. It's yours. Just don't leave your mother and sister destitute."

It's yours. And ever since, Owen had been battling with all his might to make it his.

"I haven't exactly followed in my father's footsteps," he told Gillian. "He and I still fight."

"It must be hard for you."

"Not really, not any more."

"Even though you despise the way he ran the business?"

"Gillian." He brushed his fingers against her mouth to silence her. "You're the one who despises my father's business practices. I don't necessarily go along with them, but... He's my father. My blood."

"Help me to understand," she implored. "Help me not to despise him."

Owen heard the fear in her voice, the anguish. He pulled her closer, cushioning her head against his shoulder. "He's my father. He gave me life. He fed me, sheltered me, educated me. He tried to shape me one way and I turned out a different way. But every battle I had with him forced me to analyze my position and make sure I could justify it to myself. Every argument we had taught me how to think a little better. I'm grateful to him." His fingers moved up and down her arm. Even at her elbow her skin was smooth and satiny. "Just because you disagree with a person doesn't mean you can't love him."

She sighed. Her fingers trailed down below his rib cage. The muscles of his abdomen tensed in expectation of her touch, and tensed even more when she lived up to that expectation, streaking across his skin to his navel, to his groin and then upward once more. A heated shiver rippled through his nervous system.

He wanted her. So much. Too much.

He rolled with her, rising above her and pressing her down into the mattress. His hand brushed something, and he glanced beyond her to discover the rose he'd given her, balanced precariously on the edge of the bed. She must have dropped it there when he'd carried her into the room.

He lifted the stiff green stem and touched the teardrop-shaped red bud to the tip of her nose. Smiling, she reached to take the flower, but he drew it away. He abandoned all thoughts of his father, her father, the disagreements that might in time challenge his love for her or hers for him. He focused only on now, on this magnificent, beautiful woman stretched out half beside him and half beneath him, peering up at him, her green eyes dancing with curiosity and delight.

He focused on the rose in his hand.

He wielded it like a paintbrush, a whisper of red petals against her skin. He stroked the blossom under her chin, along her throat, down the hollow between her breasts. Her eyes never left him, even as her breath caught and her body twitched in delicious discomfort.

He touched the bud to one breast and then the other. Her nipples swelled and flushed a red to match the rose. The flower's fragile perfume lingered on her skin.

He stroked the rose lower, down to her belly. At last Gillian closed her eyes; a hushed moan escaped her. "Don't," she whispered an instant before he did what she was begging him not to do, what he knew she wanted him to do. Even as she mouthed the word *no,* she shifted her thighs and bent her knees, murmuring his name on a broken sigh as he brushed the rose against her, blossom petals to petals of skin, the fragrances of flower and woman blending as her body shuddered in delight.

Simply watching her response, watching her skin glow with arousal, watching her breasts rise and fall with each hard-earned breath and her head roll back to expose the pale, graceful curve of her throat, excited him in an amazing way. Every cell in his body seemed attuned to her as he moved the rosebud again and again over her most vulnerable flesh. He held his breath when she did, felt the muscles along his spine grow tight, felt his hips surge as hers did. When at last she reached up and gripped his upper arms, digging her nails into him, gasping and trembling violently as she climaxed, he almost came with her.

He tossed the rose aside and bowed to kiss her. She released his arms and reached lower, circling him, gliding over him as her tongue glided over his lips, his teeth. She was still trembling, still panting, and he was desperately ready for her.

To his surprise, she resisted, nudging him away, forcing him onto his back. She lifted the rose and gazed down at him, a wicked glint animating her green eyes.

She was going to take revenge—and he sure as hell wasn't going to stop her.

The rose felt almost too dainty on his thicker, tougher skin—but knowing where it had spent the past few minutes was enough to excite him. She traced his nipples, teasing them into stiffness, then slid the flower along his rib cage and under his arm.

It tickled, but he suppressed his reflexive laughter. If he laughed she might stop.

She skimmed the flower downward and poked the tip into his navel. That tickled, too, but he felt no urge to laugh this time. The muscles in his thighs were so taut they ached. His lungs ached. His manhood ached. She guided the flower lower, over him, under him, twirling around him until the pain threatened to consume him.

He reached for her, but she eluded his grasp and instead bowed over him, her hair cascading around her lovely face, thick, tawny waves raining down onto his stomach and thighs. Her lips were as delicate as the rose, but moist, so moist, and her tongue...

He heard himself release a harsh, throaty cry of agony, and then he was taking her in his arms, hauling her onto him, spreading her legs around him, clamping his hands on her hips and pulling her down.

He still wanted to stay inside her forever. But not this time. Not when she was so tight, so hot and wet and heavenly. Not when she propped herself up on her arms so her breasts skimmed tantalizingly against his chest and her hair spilled down around his face, and her thighs were so strong and smooth sandwiching his hips. Not when she kept rocking against him, drawing him deeper and deeper and moaning as her body fluxed and surged and erupted in dazzling undulations all around him.

Someday he would make it last forever. But not this time.

With a smile, with a sign of resignation, with a ragged groan of ecstasy, he let go.

"No, I won't fire Sam Chappell," Owen said irritably.

Ben eyed him above the rim of his coffee cup. It was eight-twenty, and Ben had been nattering about Sam Chappell from the moment they'd been served their coffee in the cheery hotel dining room.

"You're not looking at the situation objectively," Ben said, adopting his I'm-older-and-wiser tone of voice. "You're tired, you've got bags under your eyes, and you're in no condition to do any heavy thinking. I don't know what you were up to last night, although I hope it was more fun than what I was doing."

Owen took a long, scalding sip of black coffee. Better to burn his tongue than blurt out why he was in no condition for heavy thinking. If he was in a foul mood this morning, it was only because he wished he could have awakened at sunrise with Gillian in his arms and done some more of what he'd been doing last night.

But he hadn't dared to spend the night with her. At four in the morning, when the sky was still as black as midnight, he'd slipped out of her bed, kissed away her protests and explained that he had an eight o'clock breakfast scheduled with a Moore Enterprises executive. "My father sent him to keep an eye on me," he'd told her. "I don't think he's quite ready to handle the news that I'm sleeping with the enemy."

Gillian had looked wounded. "Is that what I am? The enemy?"

"Ben thinks your father is. Just as I'm sure your father thinks I am," he'd hastened to add, cutting off her objection. "Are you in any hurry to tell your father we're lovers?"

"No," Gillian had conceded, then laughed sadly. "My father wants me to hook up with Perry Royerson."

"Who?"

"Perry Royerson. I introduced you to him at my aunt's house."

"Oh. Right. The hunk."

"He's not a hunk. He's a pediatrician."

Owen had smiled grimly. "He's a hunk *and* a pediatrician? That's tough competition."

"He's also very nice," she had goaded, her eyes twinkling with mischief.

"But you're in love with me." Owen silenced her. She'd told him she loved him, and he believed it. And believing it, he had suddenly discovered that he wasn't the least bit worried about nice, hunky Dr. Perry Royerson.

Sam Chappell, however, was a genuine cause for worry. "Will you tell your father about me?"

Gillian had met Owen's probing gaze. Her eyes had been clear even at that bleary hour. As Owen donned his trousers and reached for his shirt, she'd lain naked and tempting across her bed, her hair a voluptuous tangle of waves, her body a sculpture of enticing curves. He'd had to call upon his complete supply of willpower to keep from tearing off his clothes and making love with her one more time.

"Yes," she'd vowed. "Not right away, but I will tell him."

"When?"

"When I think he can handle it."

"Which might be sometime in the next century," Owen had muttered. "At the very least, it won't be until he retires—and then only if he decides his pension is adequate."

"It had better be adequate. I don't want to have to support him in his old age."

"You won't have to," Owen had assured her, his tone wry. "He takes care of himself very well."

"What's that supposed to mean?"

Owen hadn't wanted to get into a quarrel with her. But her wary gaze had refused to release him. "It means," he'd said carefully, "that your father knows how to make the union work to protect its members. Even if I wanted to change the pension program—which I don't—your father would make sure I didn't. For all I know, you'd help him."

"If I had to, I would."

"It's not going to happen. I'm not going to—"

"You may not think much of unions," she'd snapped, far too awake for his peace of mind, "but they serve a vital function. My mother's people were coal miners in West Virginia—her grandfathers, her father, her brothers. They had no protection before the United Mine Workers helped them. They died in explosions, they died of black lung, they went blind, they developed arthritis, and until the union came along they could barely afford to feed their families on what they earned. My mother grew up in a four-room cabin with a tin roof. They couldn't afford an indoor toilet until the United Mine Workers made it possible for her father to earn a decent wage."

"All right." Owen had stroked her arm gently. "I don't need a speech, Gillian."

"I think you do. My mother," she'd continued, her voice growing low and taut, "died when I was four years old."

"Gillian—"

"She died because she took a job in a non-union chemical plant that didn't obey all the safety regulations. There was no union representation, and if you complained to management about the fumes, you were told to shut up or quit. She and my father were saving up to buy a house. So she shut up. She worked the night shift so she could be home with me during the day. One night there was a malfunction in the ventilation system, and the plant lacked a proper alarm system, and three people inhaled too much of the fumes. Two of them survived. The third one was my mother."

"Gillian." He'd pulled her into his arms and held her, comforting. "I'm sorry. That's terrible. It's wrong. It shouldn't have happened."

"But it did. It happened because there was no union."

"I'm not going to touch your father or his union," he had whispered, stroking back her hair and kissing her brow. "I promise, Gillian. I promise."

"THIS UNION CRAP," Ben continued as the waiter set a platter of fresh fruit salad in front of him. "Maybe I could live with the union if Chappell weren't running it. He's the one who really has me concerned. Did you read through the stuff Harvey Shoup faxed over?"

"I thumbed through it."

"The man's trouble. Everywhere he goes he starts something."

"He hasn't caused trouble at Sandifer."

"Sandifer's old owners were morons. Look at how cheap they sold the company to us."

"The business returned a consistently strong profit under their management."

"We'll do better. My suggestion is that we put in our own vice president of marketing, our own vice president of manufacturing, and then we go to the union and say we all want to be one big, happy family. Or a team. That's the buzzword these days, isn't it? We'll say we want to work with labor as a team. That would decommission Chappell. He's not a team player."

"Leave it be, Ben. We're new here. Let's just let the company do what it does before we start stepping all over people's egos. Sam Chappell can be our ally if we handle things correctly."

Ben gave him a patronizing look. "Don't be naive."

"Don't be cynical," Owen retorted, emboldened by the kick of caffeine in his blood. "Times have changed, Ben. A generation ago labor and management didn't trust each other. No law says things have to stay that way."

"You don't know what you're talking about."

"Maybe I don't." Owen set down his cup and studied the man across the table from him. As much as he had always admired Ben, as grateful as he was for Ben's support and friendship over the years, Owen could not let Ben's counsel deafen him to his own.

If he couldn't persuade Ben to give in, he would have to force him. "I'm the boss, Ben," he said quietly. "So we'll do it my way."

Ben appeared nonplussed, his supercilious expression fading. "Can we at least talk to Harvey Shoup about the material he sent us?"

"Sure, we can talk. When is he free?"

"He's in court most of the day, but he said he could meet us for dinner tonight."

Owen smiled thinly. "Sorry, Ben," he said, feeling not the slightest bit sorry. "I've got plans for tonight."

"SORRY," GILLIAN SAID, meaning it, "but I've got plans for tonight."

The silence on Perry's end of the phone saddened her. "Some other time, maybe?" he asked hopefully.

She sighed. "Look, Perry— I like you. You're a great guy, and if I'd met you two years ago I'd say yes to anything. I mean that."

"Two years ago?"

Perry deserved her honesty. But she couldn't divulge the truth about her and Owen to an acquaintance of her father's.

More than an acquaintance. Her father seemed to have appointed himself Perry Royerson's champion. He had phoned Gillian the day after the barbecue and asked whether she'd heard from Perry yet. "He was quite taken with you, Gillian," her father had crowed, "even though you had to leave Lettie and Charlie's early, with that lousy headache. After you left, Perry told me he thought you were something special and said he intended to give you a call."

Now he was calling. She sat in her office, staring at the framed poster of Verona's Arena that she'd wheedled out of a travel agent. Remembering what had happened to her in the dark, arching corridors of the Arena, she tried to figure a way to explain her situation to Perry without lying. "I became involved with someone two years ago," she said, aware that was too little of the truth, and far too much.

"Your father told me you were unattached."

"I was. But the man . . . well, just recently he reappeared, and . . ." And he captivated her. Beguiled and bedeviled her. Acquired her heart and soul while he was busy acquiring Sandifer Chemicals.

"I understand," Perry said coolly.

She wished she could believe him. "Listen, Perry— I've got a terrific girlfriend I could set you up with."

"Thanks, anyway. I can find my own dates."

"She's a lawyer on Wall Street and she's gorgeous."

"Gillian, really—"

"She's got a great sense of humor, and she's bright, and—I'm not kidding—she turns people's heads, she's so pretty."

"I'm not shopping around, Gillian," he said. "I don't like blind dates. I agreed to meet you because your father and I hit it off. I still happen to like your father. I was hoping there might be possibilities for you and me, but maybe it won't work out. So . . . I guess I'll say goodbye."

She heard a click as he hung up. A strange melancholy hovered over her, not just because she'd apparently bruised the ego of a charming man, but because the friendship between Perry and her father could never exist between Owen and her father.

She loved her father. She wanted him to love the man she loved. But it wasn't going to happen, at least not for a long, long time. Not until her father was absolutely convinced that Owen wouldn't do things the way his father had done them in the past.

That might take years.

Even worse, it might take years for Gillian to learn that perhaps Owen *did* do things the way his father had done them. He had insisted that he wouldn't, but he'd also said he loved his father, a man she abhorred on principle. If Owen could love a man like Franklin Moore, what else might he be capable of?

If only she could have been receptive to Perry Royerson, if only she could have been attracted to him. Life would have been so simple.

But she couldn't force herself to like him. For two years she hadn't been able to force herself to like any man. She'd gone on dates, attended parties, let her cousin Amy pass along her number to some of her ex-boyfriends. Nothing had taken, nothing had worked.

And Owen was the reason.

Gillian let her mind drift back to the night she'd spent with him, a night during which the heat he'd kindled with a few audacious kisses in Verona, Italy, finally burst into flames in Verona, New Jersey. Merely recalling his kisses, his touch, his intimacy made her uncomfortably warm and restless, yearning for more.

What other man could have given her as much as Owen had last night?

To what other man could she have given so much of herself?

How much more would they be able to give each other before he returned to California? Before the man Owen's father had sent to check up on Owen found out that he was sleeping with the enemy, as he'd put it? Before her own father found out?

She would see him tonight, and tomorrow night, and every night until he went home. And then . . .

Then he would be three thousand miles from her, living in Venice while she lived in Verona. She recalled the distance between Verona and Venice in Italy. The train ride had taken less than two and a half hours, yet it had carried her thousands of miles and two years from her own happiness.

Was Owen going to leave Verona for Venice the way she had? Was he going to leave her staring after him, wondering when she would ever see him again? She couldn't bear the thought that their love was doomed. Touching the statue was supposed to bring luck in love.

Maybe the statue had brought them luck in love. But was it good luck or bad?

Chapter Eleven

"As a lover," Romeo observed, rather admiringly, "he is most inventive."

"Inventive and tender, like you."

"It seems impossible that he might love her as much as I love you."

"I do not question that you love me as much as a man can love a woman. But can we not see the same degree of love in him? Observe how he gazes upon her, how he holds her with such gentle reverence. It is more than affection, more than hunger. What brings them together is love." Juliet smiled with satisfaction. "I consider this a marvelous triumph."

"And I consider your conclusion premature. Your chosen lovers still face many obstacles."

How like Romeo to assume the worst. "What obstacles, pray tell? Do you believe that after their sublime congress they shall end up toasting each other with poison or plunging daggers into their hearts? Look at him. Look at her. The air shimmers with their love—a love that can lead only to a happy ending."

"You are too smug, my lady. The air in Gillian's bed chamber may shimmer with their love, but ominous

*winds blow outside her door. What shall happen once
the world learns of this secret love?''*

"What shall happen is peace," Juliet replied, although she wondered whether Romeo's doubts held
validity. "Imagine, sweet Romeo, a world that can embrace the goodness of love, that can let it shed its glorious light into every dark corner. Imagine a world that
can celebrate when two people discover the joy of such
a love. Imagine a world in which Gillian's father and
Owen's can shake hands and accept each other as family. 'My daughter loves your son, and that is good
enough for me,' her father might say. 'Hail, my
brother,' his father will rejoin, 'for the love of our dear
children casts its spell upon us all and melts the iciest of
hearts.'''

"I have always admired your imagination," Romeo
declared. "Would that it were more closely connected
to reality...."

"If what I imagine cannot come true, the fault lies
not in my imagination, Romeo, but in those who deny
the magnificent vision it offers. Anything is possible if
there but be enough love."

"I shall not dispute that Gillian and Owen have
love," Romeo conceded. "But enough love? Who can
know if they have enough?"

"They themselves, my husband. They alone can
know whether it is enough."

"ONE OF THESE DAYS," Owen whispered hoarsely,
"we're really going to have to slow down."

He was holding her in his lap, with her legs wrapped
like a belt around his waist and his forehead resting
wearily against hers. Her hands were still locked around

his shoulders, her breath still coming in great, uneven gulps.

"Slow down?" she managed once she'd regained control of her breathing. "Why?"

He laughed and trailed his fingers down her back to her bottom. Cupping her in his palms, he kneaded the round flesh until her hips gave an involuntary twitch of pleasure. "We tear off our clothes and go at it like a couple of horny kids."

"I never did anything like this when I was a kid," she said haughtily. "I was pretty modest in my youth."

"And now you're making up for lost time?" he teased, wedging his hands under her and lifting her higher. His tongue flicked over one of her nipples and the other, and then he buried his lips in the warm hollow between her breasts. "I want to make love to you so slowly it takes hours," he murmured, "and by the time we're done we're so drained neither of us can move, or talk, or think." He lowered her back into his lap and kissed her lips. "The trouble is, I stop thinking the instant I'm inside you. I lose my self-control. You feel too good." He kissed her again, a longer, deeper kiss. "It's never been like this before, Gillian. Never."

It had never been like this for her, either. Merely listening to him talk about what they'd just experienced filled her with a fresh surge of arousal. She wanted to rub against him, make him hard again, bind their bodies together and lose herself in the savage ecstasy of his lovemaking.

She wanted to stop thinking.

When she thought, she thought about all the difficulties lying in wait beyond her bed, beyond the sacred darkness of their shared night. Difficulties like their fathers, their backgrounds, their homes on opposite sides of the country.

She didn't want to talk about any of it, didn't want to think about it—but it was there, demanding acknowledgment. Just because Owen could make her feel sensations she'd never even dared to dream about didn't make all the problems disappear.

"What are we going to do?" she asked.

Owen didn't answer right away. Her words lingered in the air, a distant echo of the words he'd spoken in the gloomy corridor of the Arena so long ago. *What are we going to do?*

"We'll go to Venice," he finally said.

"Italy?"

"California." He leaned back far enough so they could see each other squarely. "Come home with me. Marry me."

Marry him. Oh, God, she wanted to. She loved him so much; she couldn't bear the thought of not spending the rest of her life with her arms and legs curled around him, the way they were right now.

But California?

Her work was here, her career, and the people who had made that career a reality, who had helped her to realize her ambitions. Her family had encouraged her, they'd pushed her and they'd all taken pride in her accomplishments. Uncle Charlie had hired her to wash his car, not because he couldn't do a better job himself but because he wanted to be able to contribute to her college funds without making her feel she was accepting charity. Aunt Lettie had lent her a typewriter and had proofread all her college applications. Amy—two years younger, but with a far more sophisticated fashion sense—had helped her assemble a wardrobe initially for college and later for her first job with the state labor council.

Her family. That was the real reason she couldn't go to California. The Chappell family was a small but tightly knit clan. They got together frequently, casually, for birthdays and holidays, for grilled burgers and televised play-off games. They talked to each other, badgered each other, interfered in each other's lives. Loved each other.

How could she move to California, three thousand miles from them? She was her father's only child; he was her only parent.

Of course she could telephone him regularly if she moved. And she could fly east to visit him once or twice a year. . . .

Tears welled up in her eyes. When she blinked them away enough to see clearly, she found Owen frowning.

"I want to marry you," she said, wanting only to erase the wariness in his expression.

"But . . ."

"But California."

"It's not so far. They even speak English there."

"This is where I live, Owen. Verona."

"New Jersey." He wrinkled his nose.

"New Jersey is a wonderful place. It's my home. You can't possibly claim that Verona isn't a lovely town."

"The only lovely thing about Verona is that you're here. Gillian, please—I want you with me. I've got a beautiful house a block from the beach. The weather is gorgeous all year round. You can take the California bar exam and become licensed to practice there. I've got lots of business connections—I could help you find a position with a Los Angeles law firm if you'd like."

"Let me think about it," she hedged, lowering her eyes and pulling him back into her arms. The truth was, she *didn't* want to think about it. Thinking about it—thinking about saying goodbye to her father and her home, or goodbye to Owen—was unbearable.

So she did what she knew would make it impossible for either of them to think. She pressed Owen back against the pillow and covered his mouth with hers and lowered herself into his powerful, protective arms. She moved against him, slithered, writhed, stroked, awakened him until his body was hers, moving to her rhythm, at her speed. She seduced him with her passion, her tenderness, her love.

And for that moment, at least, they both stopped thinking.

HER PHONE RANG. She lay where she was, in his arms, languid and heavy and so comfortable he didn't want to release her. Peering past her at the alarm clock on her night table, he saw that it was nearly ten.

The phone rang again. "Aren't you going to answer it?"

"The machine will get it," she said drowsily.

He smiled and sent a silent thank-you to whoever invented answering machines. Any technology that enabled him to keep Gillian in his arms was all right with him.

The machine clicked on and a voice emerged through the speaker. "Gillian? It's Dad. Kind of late for you to be out on a weeknight, but I'm hoping it's because you're having such a good time with Perry Royerson. He told me he was going to call you today, and I guess he did. I'm real happy you two hit if off. Well, sweetheart, call me tomorrow and fill me in."

Another click, and the room filled with silence.

"The nice pediatrician," Owen recalled.

"He's my father's fantasy. Not mine."

"What's yours?" Owen asked. *Say it's me. Say your fantasy is to marry me, to be with me until the end of time.*

She stirred in his arms, then eased herself off him and sat. He gazed up at her, mesmerized by her lush mane of hair, the deep sea green of her eyes, the delicate curve of her lips. "My fantasy," she said, "is for you to give up Venice for Verona."

"Verona? New Jersey?"

She nodded, her gaze brimming with hope.

He let out a long breath. Things could be worse, he supposed. At least she wanted him in her life. Although she hadn't exactly said she *would* marry him, she'd said she wanted to.

But—cripes, New Jersey? A state full of incomprehensible, unnavigable highways and turnpikes? A state full of chemical plants and smoke-belching factories and intractable unions?

Sure, Verona was a cute, little town. It had a bar and a church and Gillian. What more did he need?

He needed California. His life, his home, his ocean, his family.

If he moved to New Jersey, he could still visit his folks. They couldn't visit him—at least not his father, who became impatient with the rigmarole involved in simply getting him into his wheelchair-adapted van to travel downtown, let alone to the airport and onto a plane. If Owen lived in New Jersey, he could abandon Moore Enterprises to Ben and Marc Utrecht...and they could turn it back into the bloodthirsty organization it used to be. The first thing they'd do, probably, would be to give Gillian's father and his colleagues the ax.

"If I stayed in New Jersey," he said slowly, testing her, "you would have to tell your father about me."

"If you stayed in New Jersey, I would."

Meaning, if he left New Jersey she wouldn't?

He'd heard the message her father had left on her answering machine. Those few sentences gave him a good idea of why she wasn't eager to explain to her father the truth about Owen. Her old man wanted her to hook up with a nice pediatrician, someone he knew and trusted. Someone he himself had selected for her.

"I don't know, Gillian." Owen sighed. "I don't know."

"I can't imagine fitting into the California life-style. It's so hip and cool and live-for-the-moment."

That was a ridiculous stereotype, and he answered in kind. "Right. And New Jersey's polluted and crowded and blue collar."

"It is." She sat straighter, defiant. "That's who I am, Owen—the product of a polluted, crowded, blue-collar world. Do you still want to marry me?"

"Yes. Maybe it's not hip and cool, and it sure as hell isn't just for the moment. But yes, I do want to marry you."

She settled back into his arms. "How will we make it work?"

"We'll think of something." He ran his hand down her side to the swell of her hip, to the curve of her thigh and forward.

"If you do that, we're not going to think at all," she warned, although she didn't push his hand away.

His fingers danced through the inviting curls of hair between her legs. "We'll think later," he decided.

That was his last lucid thought for a long time.

"GILLIAN, WHERE HAVE you been?" her father asked. "I left a message on your phone last night, and one the night before. Not that I don't respect your privacy and all, but honey, if you make yourself too available to Perry, he's not going to respect you."

Gillian let out a long breath and rubbed the fingertips of her free hand against her temple, trying to massage away an incipient headache. She had to attend a settlement conference in less than a half hour, and she needed to review her notes before she faced the other side's attorney over the bargaining table.

She could hardly concentrate. Owen's marriage proposal loomed too brightly before her, making everything else insignificant and indistinct. And who could possibly think after three sleepless nights in a row?

Four, she amended. The first night after she'd found Owen in the staff lounge at Sandifer Chemicals she hadn't slept either. Not because she'd spent the night in the throes of rapturous passion, but because she'd been haunted with a worry bordering on panic.

Why was he in her life? How was she going to retain her sanity now that he was?

What are we going to do?

The worry was still there. That she and Owen loved each other ought to have simplified matters, but it didn't. She was going to have to tell her father the truth. Soon.

For his part, Owen had told the Moore Enterprises executive his father had sent to spy on him that he should return to Los Angeles alone, that Owen had to stay on in New Jersey a few extra days to tie up some personal matters. Within a day, or at most two, though, Owen was also going to have to leave for California.

It wasn't as if everything had to be settled between him and Gillian before he departed. But once he was gone, she didn't know how she was going to be able to function, let alone plan her future with him.

They were going to have to make some decisions. She would have to decide between her job and her family, on one hand, and Owen on the other. He was going to have to decide between his job and his family and her.

It was enough to make her want to run off to Italy.

"Can I see you tonight?" her father asked. "Or are you going somewhere with Perry again?"

"I'm sorry, Dad. But I do have plans for tonight." After Owen was gone she would tell her father. She wasn't about to waste time visiting her father during the few precious nights she had left with Owen.

"You're seeing him every night, Gillian. It sounds serious."

"It is." That much was the truth, at least.

"Well. You know I want what's best for you. He seems like a good man, and you're an adult. Just don't do anything stupid, okay?"

"I love you, Dad," she said, subduing the tremor in her voice. "I've got to go." She lowered the telephone into its cradle and let out a shaky sigh.

Don't do anything stupid? Hell, she'd fallen in love with a man her father hated on sight. How stupid could you get?

SHE FELT A BIT LESS stupid several hours later, at the conclusion of what had been a spectacularly successful negotiating session. The sexual-harassment class-action suit would not go to trial, after all; the company had

agreed to set up a series of values workshops for the
company's male staff, and to pay each of the women
named in the suit a generous sum. The contingency fee
Gillian earned for her law firm was nice, but she was far
more satisfied to know that she'd put a gang of insen-
sitive bosses in their place, that she'd won for the
workers.

The summer drizzle dampening the late afternoon air
caused her car's battery to balk, but it didn't dampen
her spirits. She wiped the leads dry, got the engine
started, turned on the windshield wipers and the radio.
A Pointer Sisters song filled the car and Gillian sang
along. "Romeo and Juliet," they crooned, and Gillian
thought of Verona, *her* Verona, the Verona where, in
less than two hours, she would be with Owen. The
singers moaned about how kissing set them on fire, and
Gillian smiled.

Arriving back at her office, she'd found a message on
her desk. *Call Nancy Burdette. Urgent.*

That final word smothered all the proud pleasure
she'd been feeling in the aftermath of her successful
settlement and all her giddy anticipation about seeing
Owen that evening. Nancy would never use the word
"urgent" unless she meant it.

Clutching the pink message slip, she crossed to her
door and shut it. Then she returned to her desk,
punched in the phone number of Shoup, Hawley and
fixed her gaze on the poster of the Arena, searching for
strength in the grand stone arches, the astonishing so-
lidity of the ancient building.

The Shoup, Hawley receptionist connected Gillian to
Nancy. "Oh, God, Gillian," Nancy wailed melodra-
matically. "I think I did something awful."

Hearing Nancy's familiar voice reassured Gillian. "What awful thing did you do?" she asked.

"Your father called me."

Gillian stopped feeling reassured. "About what?"

"About you."

Foreboding crept over her. "What about me?"

"He wanted to know how things were going with you and Perry Royerson."

Gillian closed her eyes. She couldn't bear to look at the Arena poster any more. It reminded her too vividly of her first meeting with Owen, of a hand reaching out of the shadows, touching her and changing the course of her life forever. "What did you tell him?"

"Well, I just... I mean, it was only natural for me to say, 'Perry Who?'"

Gillian swallowed. "And what did he say?"

"He knows we're best friends, Gillian. He knows we tell each other everything. So when I didn't immediately recognize the name Perry Royerson, he knew you've been seeing someone else the past few nights. He said you've been out every night—"

"I haven't. I've just been letting my machine answer for me."

"And he said you're going out again tonight, and he demanded to know who you were seeing."

"Did you tell him?"

"No!" Nancy said vehemently. "I swear I didn't. But... Oh, Gillian, he guessed."

"He guessed?"

"He said ever since Moore Enterprises bought Sandifer you've been acting like you were under a spell, and then he said actually you started acting different when Owen Moore arrived, and that night at your aunt and uncle's house you left early, and you've been busy every night since then, and if it wasn't Perry Royerson you were seeing, then it must be someone else who had entered your life around then. He put two and two together, Gillian.'' She sighed. ''My mistake was that I didn't deny it fast enough.''

Gillian swallowed again. Sooner or later, it all would have come out. Now that it had, she was simply going to have to deal with it.

''Nancy. You did nothing wrong, okay? You're under no obligation to lie for me.''

''I know, but—''

''I mean it. It wasn't your fault.''

''You don't hate me?''

''Of course not.'' She let out a long breath. Her panic ebbed, leaving behind a heavy sense of resignation. ''Owen asked me to marry him,'' she told Nancy, who let out a delighted gasp. ''And I've said . . . well, almost yes. The only stumbling blocks are the details—where we should live, who should give up their home. And our families, of course.'' She was rambling, sorting through her thoughts as she verbalized them. ''I mean, I was going to have to tell my father, anyway. I might as well get it over with.''

''Maybe he'll be happy for you,'' Nancy suggested, then groaned. ''No. He won't be. He had a conniption over the phone. He called Owen things that made me blush, and I don't blush easily.''

''He was really mad?''

''Mad is an understatement. He went ballistic.''

''I'll talk to him.''

''I'm sorry, Gillian.''

''Don't be sorry. Owen and I love each other. Be happy for us.''

''I am, Gillian. I am.''

But even as she hung up the phone and turned her gaze back to the poster, Gillian wasn't happy. This should be a thrilling event in her life, a time of rejoicing. The man she loved loved her just as deeply. He wanted to marry her. She wanted to be his bride. This was not an occasion for tears.

Yet her eyes brimmed with them, stung with them, and her heart beat in a heavy, dirgelike tempo. The man who had been the most important person in her life for the past twenty-six years hated the man who had become the most important person in her life in the past few days.

In the past two years. The seed of this predicament had been sown two years ago—not in the Arena, but in a courtyard a short walk away, a courtyard with an enchanted statue.

Gillian remembered the roses climbing the stone walls of that courtyard. And the rose Owen had brought her.

She wondered whether the seed they'd planted two years ago would grow into a beautiful rose, a blossom of love, red with passion—or into an ugly, poisonous weed that would choke all the beauty around it, that would wound with thorns and brambles, that would cause everything that came near it to shrivel and die.

HE GOT BACK TO HIS hotel room at around six, after a fruitful day finalizing an agreement with the investment banker who had impressed him the most out of all the financial wizards he and Ben had interviewed. Although making his decision and signing on with one banker removed Owen's professional reason for staying on in New Jersey, he was in a good mood.

He would see Gillian tonight, explain to her that his departure for California was imminent and force her to reach some sort of decision. If she wasn't prepared to move to California, he would persuade her to visit him there. They would pick a time—as soon as possible—and once she was out west and could see for herself how lovely Venice was, he would convince her to stay.

Everything was going to work out.

Noticing the flashing message light on his telephone, he dialed the front desk. "You have a message from Gillian Chappell," the concierge informed him. "She said she has a family problem and might not be able to see you tonight. If she can straighten things out, she'll call."

A family problem. It could be anything—but Owen knew intuitively that there was only one problem that counted, one that would compel her to leave such a vague message. If a relative was ill, she would have said so. If there had been an accident, a crisis with her aunt and uncle, she would have mentioned it in the message.

The problem was her father. Her father, who hated Owen.

After thanking the concierge, he requested an outside line and called her at home. After several rings, her machine switched on. He shouted that if she was there she should pick up the phone. He heard nothing but the beeps of her machine announcing that his time was up.

He scanned the documents scattered across the motel-decor desk. Page after page teemed with tales of Sam Chappell's dirty deeds, his troublesome work history, his surly resistance to management. But none of the files contained his home address or phone number.

Owen phoned Sandifer Chemicals. A security guard answered and said that only a skeleton night shift was at the plant, and Sam Chappell wasn't among them.

He phoned Directory Assistance and asked for the number of a Chappell family in Maplewood. He had no idea what town Sam Chappell lived in, but perhaps he could find out from Gillian's aunt and uncle. No one answered there—not even a machine.

He phoned Shoup, Hawley. No answer.

Rummaging through the papers on his desk, he found Harvey Shoup's business card, with his home number penned across the back. He dialed.

At last, a live voice. "Yes?"

"Harvey? This is Owen Moore."

"Owen! Hi! What can I do for you?"

"I need the home number of one of your associates. Nancy Burdette."

"Ah. Nancy. She's something, isn't she."

Owen chose to let Harvey believe what he wanted about Owen's interest in Nancy. "She's something, all right. Do you think she'd mind terribly if I called her at home?"

"She's a big girl. If she minds, she'll let you know." Harvey supplied the phone number and told Owen to be in touch if he needed anything else.

Owen hung up, took a deep breath and dialed Nancy's number. He wasn't sure what he'd do if she wasn't home.

Fortunately, she was. "Hello?"

"Nancy Burdette? This is Owen Moore."

"Oh." She said nothing for a minute. "Congratulations. I think."

Congratulations? Was Gillian's "problem" something worth celebrating?

"Gillian told me you two were talking marriage."

"Yes. We're talking." Not that they'd reached any conclusions yet, not that Gillian had said anything beyond "I'd like to marry you." "She left a message for me at my hotel, that there was a family problem," he told Nancy. "No one answered at her house, and I was hoping you might know if it's anything serious."

Nancy swore under her breath. "I hope it's not serious, but I don't know." Another curse, and then a sigh. "I don't know if I should tell you. I'm so sick of playing the go-between."

"I owe you. You can be in the bridal party. Now, please tell me what the problem is with Gillian."

"Her father knows about you."

"What do you mean, he knows about me?"

"He knows about you and her. He's pretty upset about it."

"I see."

"My guess is, Gillian's with him now. Probably trying to talk him down."

"Where does her father live?" Owen asked.

"No, Owen. If she wanted you there, she would have said so."

"She shouldn't have to tell him about us all alone. I should be by her side."

"No." Nancy sounded adamant. "You don't know what grief she gave me the other day, because I told you where her aunt lived. I'm not going to make the same mistake twice."

"Nancy." His mind scrambled for an effective argument. "All right, she gave you grief. But that was before she realized she was in love with me. Now she does realize it. I ought to be with her when she breaks the news to her father."

Another silence. "What is it with you, Owen? Why are you always trying to weasel information out of me?"

"Because you always have the information I need. I have to go and meet her father face to face and hash this thing out with him. It has to be done—and I can do it if you tell me where he lives."

"Irvington," Nancy capitulated, sounding miserable. "Her father lives in Irvington."

He grabbed a pen and scribbled the address onto a sheet of hotel stationery. Nancy recited Sam Chappell's telephone number, too, and Owen wrote it down. He thanked her, listened with sympathy as she moaned that she hoped Gillian would forgive her, and told her how indebted he was. Then he hung up.

He stared at Sam Chappell's telephone number for a moment. He couldn't call. If Gillian was at her father's house, she wasn't going to be at liberty to talk to him. And he certainly didn't want to talk to Sam on the phone. The differences they had needed to be resolved in person.

Loosening his tie, he scooped up the keys to his rented car, read the address one more time and headed down the stairs to find out from the concierge where Irvington, New Jersey, was.

THE STREET WAS GLOOMY, the houses lining the road narrow and shabby and the few trees standing along the curb large enough to block out what little evening light there was. Owen couldn't guess what colors the houses might once have been; their walls had faded to a uniform pallor, their asbestos shingles offering only a hint of yellow here, green or gray there. They were two- and three-story structures, some with peaked roofs and some with flat roofs, some with teetering front porches and some with several doorbells lined up alongside the front door, indicating that the buildings had been divided into apartments. The vest-pocket front yards were varied in quality; some displayed the results of painstaking gardening, while others were overgrown or dying.

Sam Chappell's front yard was neither gorgeous nor decrepit. The grass was a scruffy mix of brown and green, limp from the constant drizzle. The house, a white clapboard with a flat tar roof, looked as sturdy and immutable as the man who dwelled within it. There were no signs of a decorator's touch, no shutters, no flowers bordering the front walk. A lidded aluminum garbage pail stood where the concrete driveway ran between Sam's house and the house next door. Long strands of grass grew through cracks in the pavement.

Owen strolled up the walk to the front door. Through an open window he heard Sam's voice and Gillian's in a heated counterpoint. He pressed the doorbell, but it didn't seem to be working. He heard no chime or buzz through the window.

He rapped on the door, lightly and then harder. Gillian and her father's voices drowned out Owen's knock.

Shielding his eyes, he peered through the open window. It was draped in a diaphanous curtain, but he could see Gillian's shadow moving in and out of an arched doorway that opened to a room at the rear of the house. He strained to make out her words and managed to latch onto a few of them. "…makes me happy. He…"

And Sam's voice, "…don't care…remember who you are, girl. That's all that counts…"

"Maybe you should think about who I am, Dad. I'm an adult. A woman."

"You come from my people and your mother's."

"*Come from.* But where I'm going is what counts."

"You're going to hell in a hand basket. So what if you've got some fancy schooling. You think a rich hot-shot like him could be serious about someone as real and down-to-earth as you?"

Owen abandoned the front door, strode to the driveway and headed for the back of the house. The shoulders of his beige jacket grew damp and his hair, weighed down with raindrops, flopped onto his forehead. Maybe he should have changed his clothes before he'd left the hotel. But he'd thought he would make a more respectable impression if he came dressed in a suit.

A wet, wrinkled suit wasn't going to make much of an impression at all. But then, Sam didn't sound particularly receptive to any impression Owen might make.

A porch ran the width of the house in back, rising from a small cement patio in four steps. Owen detoured around the cellar door and up the steps. Although an overhang protected the sagging porch, the boards were damp and slick from the humidity.

He moved past an old barbecue grill and a pair of wrought-iron chairs padded with plastic cushions, and approached the screen door. Through it he saw a cozy kitchen with yellow counters and a green tile floor. An old table occupied the center of the room; Gillian and Sam prowled around it, pausing to yell at each other and then pacing, yelling and pacing again.

She looked beautiful. Even caught in what had to be a trying situation, Gillian radiated intelligence and conviction. Her long legs carried her purposefully around the small room; her gorgeous hair framed her face in rippling waves; her chin was held high and her eyes remained tenaciously on her father.

Sam, too, appeared strong and purposeful and full of conviction. Watching as father and daughter faced off,

Owen could see the acute resemblance between them, the pugnacious jawlines, the piercing eyes, the utter certainty in their contradictory positions.

"Your mother was killed by people like him," her father raged.

"My mother was killed by greedy bastards," she shot back. "I won't deny that. But Owen isn't one of them. He's different."

"He's the same. You are what you are. He is what he is. Maybe you went to college and law school and got yourself a fancy job, but that doesn't change who you are. He's using you, sweetheart, using you to keep me quiet. Can't you see that?"

"He isn't using me—"

"Gillian, open your eyes. Use your brain. I'm not saying you're not the greatest girl in the world—you are. But Owen Moore isn't the sort of guy who's got the taste to notice that. He's a user. An exploiter. A boss man. He's trying to soften you up, win you over to his side so I can't fight him. And God help you, girl—I think he's succeeding."

"He isn't like that, Dad."

"How do you know? You've spent, what, a few days with him? Look at the record! Look at what his father's done to working people. He does the devil's work, Gillian. I'd see him dead before I let him hurt you."

"He's not going to hurt me, Dad. Nor you, nor working people."

"How can you trust the bastard? How can you?"

"Owen." She had spotted him through the screen door, and now she stood stock-still, staring at the door, at him.

Her father spun around. His frown took on monstrous proportions. "You've got some nerve, showing your face here!" he roared, charging at the door. "I ought to arrest you for trespassing. This is my property, mister. So get the hell off it."

Owen inhaled and grappled with his temper. He had to make this work, for Gillian's sake. If he loved her, he had to win over her father.

He opened the screen door, but before he could enter the kitchen Sam barreled out onto the porch. "I've got half a mind to kill you, Moore. You touched my daughter, you're going to answer to me."

"Dad." Gillian rolled her eyes and followed him out onto the porch. "Come on, Dad. I'm an adult. Don't defend my honor, all right?"

"This guy is scum," her father railed, waving an accusing finger at Owen. "I'm not talking about chastity here, I know what times are, I'm not talking about outdated morality. But *this* guy, this piece of dirt who makes a career of stomping on honest workers, crushing them beneath the heels of his custom-made two-hundred-dollar shoes... He's not fit to touch you, honey. He's not fit."

"Please, Dad." Her tone was low but beseeching. "Don't embarrass us all. Owen and I are in love, and I won't have you calling him names."

"It's okay, Gillian," Owen interjected. "Why don't you go inside? Your father and I can talk calmly about this."

Rolling her eyes again, Gillian shook her head. "My father doesn't know the meaning of the word calm." She edged past her father and brushed her hand lightly against Owen's arm. "You shouldn't have come. It's like pouring gasoline on a fire. You're only going to make things worse."

"I love you," he said, as if her father weren't even there. He saw only Gillian, her fine, distinct features, her stubborn chin and stubborn eyes and the lips that had loved his body, that had whispered her deepest thoughts and hopes and dreams.

The stronger she appeared, the more he wanted to protect her. He wanted to fight this fight for her, to make her father confront the truth, to let the honesty and goodness of his love for her solve every problem, smooth over every snag, remedy every discomfort.

Turning to her father, he offered a slight smile. "Mr. Chappell, let's not resort to name-calling. We're all reasonable adults—"

"Did your father teach you to say that?" Sam shot back. "I know the lingo, Moore. It's what management always says just before they screw you to the wall. 'We're all reasonable, so let's reduce your wages twenty percent. We're all reasonable, so let's do away with the company's contribution to the 401K. Times are tough, the economy is weak, we bosses have had to tighten our belts, too. We're earning only a million dollars apiece this year. So you be reasonable and cut your throats for us, okay?'"

"I'm not here to talk about wages or throats or anything else."

"You're here to tell me you want my daughter, right? Let me tell you something, Owen Moore—you may be rich, but in my eyes you're worth nothing. I don't like where you come from. I don't like your family. I think you went and romanced my daughter so she'd turn against me, so I couldn't count on her when push came to shove at the bargaining table. I think you're exactly that dishonest, Owen. And I want you off my property and out of my life. And out of Gillian's."

"Dad—"

"You stay out of it," he warned, aiming his threatening finger at Gillian. "This fight is between this money-grubbing bloodsucker and me." He stalked across the porch until he was less than an inch from Owen. They stood toe to toe and eye to eye, Sam's height matching Owen's but his body thicker and bulkier, his hands meatier. "Did you touch my daughter?"

"Oh, for God's sake!" Gillian erupted, starting toward her father.

Sam ignored her. He grabbed Owen's shirt, fisting his hand around the unbuttoned collar, around the loosened silk knot of his tie. "Did you touch her?"

Owen arched his fingers gently but firmly against Sam's thick wrist and pushed back, forcing him to release his shirt. He didn't care that Sam was Gillian's father, that her ability to accept him was intertwined with her desire not to alienate her father. The man had touched him, strong-armed him, tried to intimidate him.

Owen did not get intimidated. He got mad.

"When I touch Gillian," he said, his voice taut, bristling with fury, "it's with love. When you touch me, you're being a bully. I'll thank you not to touch me that way again."

Sam jerked his arm out of Owen's grasp. "You're calling me a bully?"

"Yes."

"Dad. Owen." Gillian must have sensed the escalating hostility between the two men. She stepped toward them, prepared to intervene. Owen turned to ward her off, and Sam swung.

Owen saw the wide arc of Sam's arm peripherally. He lifted his hand barely in time to deflect the punch with his open hand. Sam was strong; the impact of his fist against Owen's palm left it momentarily numb.

"Dad!" Gillian cried. "Stop!"

"I could kill this SOB," Sam growled. "Bad enough what your people do to my people. But what you're doing to my daughter, Moore...I could kill you for that."

He swung again, and Owen threw up an arm to block the punch. He felt the bruise against his forearm as Sam's fist slammed into it.

Damn it to hell. He didn't want to fight Gillian's father—not because Sam was older than he by some thirty years, but because of Gillian. Because he loved her. Because he'd promised not to hurt her father and he couldn't break that promise.

He had to defend himself, though. Sam grabbed Owen's right arm with his left hand to hold him steady as he wound up to swing with his right. Owen wrenched free and realized Sam's fist was flying toward his head. He reached up and shoved Sam away.

Sam's shoes skidded on the slippery boards of the porch. His foot got tangled in the legs of a wrought-iron chair and he lurched wildly, plunging backward down the steps.

He lay motionless against the broken cement of the patio, his eyes closed, his mouth agape, his hands still coiled into fists. The rain drizzled down onto his ashen face.

Gillian screamed.

Chapter Twelve

"He's still breathing," she whispered. "He's still breathing. We've got to get him to the hospital, Owen."

She was kneeling at the bottom of the steps, bowing over her father's motionless body, rubbing the raindrops from his cheeks as her own cheeks grew wetter and wetter, a mixture of rain and tears.

"Don't move him," Owen cautioned, hovering beside her. "If his neck—"

"No, I know that. I know." She was babbling, just this side of hysterical. He saw her fingers shake as she stroked them against her father's skin. "It's okay, Daddy. It's okay...." Her voice dissolved into a sob.

Hunkering down behind her, Owen cupped his hands over her shoulders and brushed a light kiss against her hair. Droplets of water were trapped in the strands, glistening like diamonds embedded in gold. "I'll get help," he said, even though he didn't want to leave her. "Is there a telephone inside?"

She nodded. "In the kitchen. Call an ambulance. There's a phone number—"

"I'll find it."

"Okay. Everything's going to be okay."

"Whatever you do," Owen cautioned, "don't move him."

"I know. I know." It was a low, keening sound, a chant, an incantation. Maybe she thought that if she said "I know" enough times, her father would come back to life.

Reluctantly, Owen straightened up, climbed the porch steps and entered the house. Through the screen door he could still see her hunched over her father, trying to shield his face from the rain that pasted her skirt to her thighs and her blouse to her back.

Owen had felt the trembling in her shoulders when he'd touched her. He'd sensed the anguish and terror emanating from her in waves of tension. He wished he could have stayed outside with her, holding her, propping her up, sharing his supply of courage with her—although he had little to spare.

Summoning an ambulance was more important.

He located the wall phone above the counter near the refrigerator. A sticker attached to the receiver listed emergency numbers.

He dialed the police. "There was an accident," he told the dispatcher. In a calm, even voice, Owen requested emergency medical assistance and recited the address. His gaze remained riveted to the screen door, to the scene beyond it. To his beloved Gillian and her beloved father.

The man he may have killed.

A wave of dread surged through him, then receded, leaving a desolate sense of resignation in its place. If he'd killed Sam Chappell, he couldn't wish the tragedy away. It had happened. It was a terrible accident, as much Sam's fault as his own, and there was no way to undo what was.

Once again, Owen felt as if his life had veered out of his control, as if fate were pulling the strings. Like everything that had occurred since the afternoon he'd touched the statue of Juliet, this was one more event, one more crisis that Owen could not have changed even if he'd tried.

He leaned against the kitchen counter, closed his eyes and prayed for God's forgiveness, and Gillian's. Another wave of dread seized him, leaving him weak and nauseated. He had hurt a man, possibly killed him.

Gillian's father.

The wave ebbed, depositing him back on solid ground. He blinked his vision clear. A blanket, he thought, recalling a first-aid course he'd taken years ago. Shock victims were supposed to be kept warm. He had to cover Sam with a blanket.

Figuring the bedrooms would be upstairs, he raced toward the stairway at the front of the house. A crocheted afghan was draped decoratively across the back of a sofa in the front parlor. He grabbed it and hurried back through the kitchen to the porch.

Gillian was cradling her father's head in her hands and rocking back and forth, her eyelashes spiked with moisture and her breath barely concealing her sobs. Owen spread the afghan over Sam's body, tucking in his arms and legs, smoothing the cover around Sam's shoes. Kneeling beside Gillian, he arched his arm around her and wondered if she would allow him to keep it there, or if she couldn't stand his touch after what he'd done.

Sighing, she let her head rest for a moment against his and closed her eyes. "He's still breathing and he's got a pulse," she said, sounding less hysterical than before. "He doesn't seem to be bleeding anywhere. I don't know what's wrong."

"An ambulance is on its way."

"Okay. Okay." She pulled out of his gentle embrace and turned to gaze at him. "You have to go now."

Even though he'd prepared himself for her hatred, it hurt to have her push him away.

"I mean it, Owen." Her voice was eerily steady, devoid of anxiety. "There'll be questions. You shouldn't be here."

He understood; she was sending him off not because she hated him but because she wanted to protect him. Her devotion to him, even after what he'd done, touched the deepest, most tender part of his soul.

He wasn't going to run away. He would face the consequences, whatever they were. "I'm staying."

"Owen." Her voice was soft but steady, her emotions carefully reined in. "Listen to me. The police are going to come. They'll file a report, they'll ask questions—"

"And I'll answer them. I did this, Gillian. I'm not going to deny it."

"It was an accident. You didn't do anything."

"I pushed him—"

"He attacked you. You were only defending yourself."

"I pushed him," Owen insisted. The ghastly instant replayed itself in his mind: the bite of Sam's fingers around his right arm, immobilizing him, and then the vicious swing of Sam's fist, Owen reflexively wrenching away, shoving Sam back before his fist made contact.

The police could ask Owen what had happened, and if he answered honestly he could tell them that at the moment he'd forced Sam back he had probably wished the old man dead.

"I pushed him," he said again, with weary finality.

"He fell. Go, Owen—please, before the police get here. I'm a lawyer. I know what they're going to ask. There's no need for you to be a part of it."

"I *am* a part of it." The central part, the worst part, the most bitter, treacherous part. The murderous part.

"There's no need," she swore. "I'll tell them what happened."

"What will you say?"

"That he slipped on the wet porch, lost his balance and hit his head. It's the truth, Owen."

"Not the whole truth."

"It's all they need to know." Her penetrating gaze met his. She looked composed, no trace of panic in her clear green eyes. "Trust me, Owen. You can't be here when the police arrive."

He sighed. He wanted to stay with her, wanted to face his doom without flinching. But Gillian had asked him to trust her.

He had no choice.

Taking her face in his hands, he pressed his lips lightly to hers and tasted the salt of her tears on her skin. "I'm going," he conceded, then stood, turned and walked away.

His intention was to drive back to the hotel in Fort Lee. But once again, the car seemed to steer its own path, carrying him where fate wanted him, where he had to be.

By now he knew his way fairly well around the town of Verona. He cruised past the bar, past the manicured middle-class houses, the neat lawns and the botanical splendor of the town park, past the stores he'd grown to recognize over the previous few days. As the traffic in front of him braked for a red light at an intersection up ahead, he glanced out his window and found himself slowing to a halt in front of the church.

The inevitability of it brought a pensive smile to his face. He parked the car and went inside.

He didn't have the church to himself this time. The flickering votive candles illuminated the Gothic interior of the chapel for at least a dozen people, some of them seated along the pews and a couple of them kneeling in prayer.

Owen took a seat at the rear of the church. He studied the carved molding of the back of the pew in front of him, the gilt trim along the edge of the choir loft, the intricacies of the narrow stained-glass windows lining the walls. He breathed in the stinging scent of wax and incense and listened to the thumping of his heart in his chest.

What if Sam Chappell died?

What if Owen was a murderer?

What would Gillian do? How would she bear it? Owen could accept his own punishment more easily than he could accept the possibility that he'd caused her such pain.

Across the aisle from him, an elderly man thumbed through his rosary beads and mumbled prayers. Owen tried to recite a prayer from his own denomination, but his mind balked. The only words he could think of were, *I'm sorry. I love you, Gillian. I'm sorry.*

"You can confess now," a woman informed him as she walked up the aisle past his pew.

Confession of the formal religious sort wasn't a part of Owen's repertory. Yet he felt the need to talk, to make sense of how things could have gone so very wrong.

Just like the last time Owen had wandered into this church, he was lost. Just like that time, he needed answers—or at least a way to endure the unanswerable questions.

He walked down the aisle to the altar and turned left to where a curtained oak booth stood in an alcove. After a moment's hesitation, he pushed aside one of the curtains and stepped into the hot, close confines of the booth. The curtain dropped shut behind him and he flinched.

"Father Lawrence?" he asked, feeling incredibly awkward. "Is that you?"

Through a translucent screen he heard a coughing noise. "It's been a while for you, hasn't it," came the priest's familiar voice. "You're supposed to begin, 'Bless me, Father, for I—'"

"I'd rather talk to you in person," Owen said, edging open the curtain so he could get a little air in the booth. "Can we take this somewhere else?"

Father Lawrence cleared his throat again. "Well, actually I was supposed to be done hearing confessions ten minutes ago. I suppose I could use a break."

Owen stepped outside his half of the booth as Father Lawrence stepped outside the other half. The priest seemed to recognize him at once. "Ah, it's you. Lost again, are you?"

"Yes."

"You're looking for Fort Lee," the priest recollected.

"Not this time."

Father Lawrence waited for Owen to elaborate. When he didn't, the priest beckoned him to a heavy wooden door that led out of the chapel. They walked together down a short hallway to an office. Father Lawrence switched on the light and waved Owen inside.

The room was small but neat. A large desk occupied most of the available space. One wall held rows of bookshelves, another a massive crucifix of carved walnut. Father Lawrence gestured to one of the upholstered chairs beside the desk and Owen sat.

"Can I get you a drink?" he asked.

Much as Owen would have relished a stiff whiskey, he thought it best to remain sober. "No, thanks."

The priest eyed him with amusement, then pulled a can of diet cola from a freezer chest beside his desk. "I'm addicted to this stuff," he said, popping the top and pouring the soft drink into a coffee mug. "My secret sin." He took a hearty swig, licked the bubbles from his upper lip and then leaned back in his chair and regarded Owen thoughtfully, his bifocals magnifying his dark, round eyes. "Now, son, tell me. What's your secret sin?"

"I think I killed a man."

The priest was obviously startled. He straightened up slowly, as if afraid to spook Owen. "You *think* you killed him?"

"It was an accident. I didn't want to hurt him. He fell and hit his head. I don't know how badly he was injured. He might be dead. I didn't stick around to find out."

"You ran away?"

"I wanted to stay, but Gillian—his daughter—told me she'd get him to the hospital and I should leave the scene."

"I see." The priest meditated for a moment, his gaze never leaving Owen. "This man...was he a friend of yours?"

Owen glanced covetously at the mug of soda. Putting the catastrophe into words seemed to parch his throat, as if the words themselves were scraping against it, rubbing it raw. "I never meant to hurt him, but he and I certainly weren't friends. He was trying to keep me and Gillian apart."

The priest tapped his fingers together as he worked through his thoughts. "Gillian is the woman from Verona," he guessed. "The one you love."

"Yes."

"So. You've chosen love over home and business?"

"I never got to make a choice," Owen replied, and realized how true that was. He hadn't chosen to hurt Sam, hadn't chosen to fight with him, hadn't chosen to antagonize him. He had never presented himself to Sam as anything but a new manager determined to make Sam's life at Sandifer Chemicals as good as it had always been, if not better.

Owen hadn't chosen any of this.

He hadn't even chosen to love Gillian. If he'd had a choice, he would have chosen a woman from California, someone whose father would have embraced him, someone who didn't carry all kinds of prejudices about who he was or where he'd come from.

But he loved Gillian. He couldn't imagine loving anyone else. If he lost her, he would never love again.

It wasn't his choice. It was simply the truth.

"Perhaps," Father Lawrence suggested, "it's time for you to make some choices."

"My first choice would be to turn myself in to the police."

"That sounds noble. And what would you tell them?"

"That . . . that Sam fell. That he tripped and fell and . . ." Owen tapered off, aware that in fact there was nothing to tell.

It wasn't his fault.

So why did he feel so damned guilty?

Shaking off his remorse, he reconsidered his answer. His first choice would be to find Gillian, to take her in his arms and kiss her and tell her that no matter what happened, they had to stay together.

"I need to be with Gillian," he said aloud.

"Then be with her."

Father Lawrence made it sound simple enough. "She's probably at the hospital with her father," said Owen.

"Which hospital?"

"I don't know."

"I guess you'll have to find out." Father Lawrence pushed his telephone across the desk toward Owen. Then he leaned back in his chair and tugged a fat telephone directory from one of the bookshelves. "There you go," he said, flipping through the yellow pages until he found a listing for hospitals. "I'm going to head back out and see if anyone else is waiting to confess. You find your woman and go to her."

Owen stood when Father Lawrence did, and shook his hand. "Thank you."

The priest smiled. "You have made a choice, you know."

"I hope it's the right one."

"God alone knows," Father Lawrence said, glancing upward. He shrugged, patted Owen's shoulder, and strode out of the office.

Owen listened to the click of the door shutting, then dropped back into the chair and stared at the listings of hospitals in Essex County. He took a deep breath, lifted the receiver and started dialing.

"GILLIAN."

The voice reached her as if through fathoms of water. She felt herself rising from her drowning despair, floating upward into the light of the waiting room. She had numbed herself to the fluorescent lights, the din of voices, the squeak of rubber-soled shoes against the linoleum floor and the rattle of wheeled carts rolling by the sofa where she sat. She'd tuned out the beepers, the constant paging: *Dr. So-and-So needed in OR. Dr. Such-and-Such, report to ICU. Would the owner of a silver Volvo, license plate blah-blah-blah, please move it from the driveway at the main entrance.*

She'd submerged herself into a deep trance. All the noise, all the activity around her was nothing more than the tide, washing over her, dragging her deeper in her own turbulent thoughts.

She loved Owen. Even now, even after this. Her father had behaved like a beast. All Owen had done was to try to keep from getting hurt, and . . .

Her father's fall played itself over again and again in her mind: the sickening heaviness of it, the suddenness, the finality. Her father, so big and robust and indestructible, tumbling down to the concrete patio and hitting it with a horrid thud, and then lying there, lifeless.

And Owen. Owen trying to shelter her, trying to comfort her, prepared to sacrifice himself for the chance to remain with her.

She'd been right to send him away. Why complicate the situation? Her father had fallen. It was an accident. *Just get him to the hospital and save his life,* she'd told the police officer who had arrived at her house with the EMS technicians. *It was a terrible fall. Let's just get him some help.*

Now she waited. Waited for the results of the X rays, the CAT scans, the surgery the neurologist said was necessary to relieve the swelling inside his skull. Too early to tell, they'd said. Too early to make any predictions.

She drew in a deep breath, as though she actually had emerged from a deep pool of water, and opened her eyes to find Perry Royerson standing in front of her.

"Perry?"

She must have looked as dazed as she felt, because he gave her a gentle smile, sat next to her on the stiff vinyl couch and sandwiched her icy hands between his large, warm ones. He had on a white coat; the ear hooks of a stethoscope protruded from a side pocket. "A patient of mine was admitted an hour ago. I came over to see how she was doing and I got to chatting with one of the residents in ER. I heard your father was here."

"Yes."

"They've got an excellent staff," Perry told her. "Your father is getting the best treatment possible."

She nodded and slid her hands from Perry's. His words were soothing, but she didn't want to be with him right now.

She wanted Owen.

It would have been bad if he'd been present when the police had arrived. He would have told the whole truth: that her father loathed Owen with a passion, that he'd accused Owen of insidious things, that ever since Owen had faced him across a table in the employee lounge her father had suspected the worst of him. That if anyone had a motive for hurting Sam Chappell, it was Owen.

And then they would have arrested him on an assault charge, maybe attempted murder, maybe—God, she couldn't bear to think of it—murder.

It *wasn't* murder. Her father had charged at Owen. Owen had resisted. That was the truth, but Gillian knew enough about criminal law to guess that the police would arrest first and figure out the details later. She'd had to send him away.

No one else could comfort her right now. Certainly not Perry Royerson.

"I'm sure they're taking good care of my father," she said. "Thanks for stopping by."

Perry refused to take the hint. "Can I get you some coffee?"

She shook her head.

"Is there anyone you want me to call? Your aunt and uncle, maybe?"

"They aren't home." She had already telephoned their house. "It's all right, Perry. I appreciate your offer of help, but—"

"Are there other relatives? Your cousins, maybe. I'll do whatever I can. Your father is a fine man, Gillian."

My father would have been happy to kill my lover, Gillian thought, then suppressed a shudder. How could she think such a thing about him when he was fighting for his life?

She could think it because it was true. And that only frightened her more.

"Thanks, Perry," she said more firmly. "There's really nothing you can do." *This isn't your problem. Please, just go away.*

A doctor dressed in green scrubs stepped into the waiting area. Pulling off his cap, he searched the room for Gillian. She rose to her feet, but Perry bounded across the room before she could take a step. "How's the patient?" Perry asked.

"Well, we've done what we could," the surgeon began, then launched into a highly technical description of the surgery he'd performed on Gillian's father. As she approached the two doctors, phrases like "cranial hemorrhage" and "neurological episode" leaped out at her.

As shaken as she was, she was infuriated by Perry's attempt to take over. "Excuse me," she said, "I'm Mr. Chappell's daughter. I'm the one you should be talking to."

"Oh—I'm sorry," the doctor said, looking sheepish. "I thought Dr. Royerson was a friend."

She swallowed her rage. She was overreacting; Perry meant no harm. "Please tell me how my father is," she requested, straining to keep her anger out of her voice. "In plain English. I'm not a doctor."

In plain English, she was told that the surgery went well but that the odds of her father surviving were impossible to gauge. She was told, in plain, blunt, painful English, that until the swelling inside his skull decreased, no one would be able to determine whether he would suffer permanent brain damage if he did survive. Obviously a freak accident, the surgeon said. How devastating that he fell with such an impact. He was going to spend the night in intensive care. By morning, perhaps, the prognosis would be clearer.

Perry curved his arm around her, as if to shield her from the surgeon's brutal words. Gillian shrugged out of Perry's embrace. She didn't want him insinuating himself into her life. He might be her father's buddy, but he was practically a stranger to her.

"Everything's going to be fine," he said.

"Everything's *not* going to be fine," she retorted. None of what had happened was his fault, but she resented his taking over, positioning himself to be her knight in shining armor. "I need to be by myself for a while," she said, turning to the surgeon. "Thank you, but I just...I need to think."

"We have counselors here," Perry offered. "Chaplains—if you'd like to talk to someone—"

As if she hadn't just announced that she wanted to be alone. "No, thanks," she said, impatience creeping into her tone. "I'll be back later." Before either of the doctors could say another word, she spun on her heel and marched out of the room.

Her skirt was still rain damp and wrinkled, gathering in clammy folds around her legs as she walked. Her shoes squeaked; the collar of her blouse lay limp against her neck. She didn't care. She had to get out of this clean, brightly lit building with its sterile aromas and concerned medical practitioners. She had to get out.

She reached the main entry, a lobby designed with an emphatic cheeriness that made her feel even more dismal. The glass doors parted automatically when she neared them and she stepped out into the humid evening. A long awning extended to the semicircular driveway; beyond it, rain fell in silvery sheets.

A dark figure grew visible through the rain. He wore a beige summer-weight suit, his tie dangling loose from his open shirt collar, his black hair plastered to his face as he stalked resolutely toward the building.

Once again, Owen was stepping out of the darkness and into her life.

She had wanted to be alone—but she wanted even more to be with him. She raced down the walk and fell into his arms.

They stood holding each other for a long time. The rain showered down on them, the night breeze wrapped around them, but they didn't move, didn't speak. They simply held on.

Finally, Owen broke the silence. "How is he?"

"I don't know."

He walked her under the awning and pulled back. With his thumb, he wiped the raindrops from her cheeks. "I killed him," he said, his voice dry and cold as his words.

"No. If he dies . . ." Her voice cracked. Merely hearing herself utter the words was agonizing.

"We have to tell the police the truth."

"The truth is, he did this to himself. He came at you, Owen. He tried to hurt you. He's too stubborn, and he's too quick to anger, and he's the most exasperating person I know." A sob filled her throat and she swallowed it back down. "Oh, God. He's my father, Owen. I love him."

"Then you can't love me," Owen said bleakly. "Not after what I've done to him."

"You didn't do it. He did it to himself."

"Because of me."

"Owen, listen." She gripped his arms, forcing him to face her. Gazing into the limitless darkness of his eyes, she saw an anguish to match her own. "It was an accident."

"Everything was an accident," he countered, his voice underlined with a quiet fury. "The fact that you and I met was an accident. The fact that we fell in love—"

"Yes," she cut him off. "We fell in love. That hasn't changed."

"Of course it's changed."

"Not for me."

He stared at her as if he didn't quite believe her.

"Not for me," she repeated.

"Even if your father dies?" He spoke deliberately, testing her faith in him, in herself, in her ability to withstand the cruelest of losses.

If her father died, she knew she would love Owen as much as it was possible for her to love a person. The real question, though, was whether she would still be capable of love.

"I have to deal with this," she said, waving vaguely toward the hospital's entry. "I can't make any promises until I know what's going to happen to my father. It doesn't mean I don't love you, Owen."

"I understand."

She sensed his withdrawal more than saw it. It was something internal, something spiritual, and it left her feeling bereft.

"If my father dies," she said, surprising herself with her bravery in acknowledging the possibility, "I'll have to deal with that, too. I'm his daughter, his only child. I can't run off to California and marry you now, Owen. I love you, but I need to be here right now."

"Yes."

"And I need to know you love me." She peered up, searching his face, almost afraid that he would say he no longer did.

His eyes were still dark, mesmerizingly dark, luring her into their infinite depths. "I love you."

She realized she'd been holding her breath. She let it out in a sigh, wondering why she felt so little relief.

"What are we going to do?" she asked, her tone low and mournful. It was their own private refrain, the sum of their relationship. When would things ever work out for them? When would their path open wide, when would their love flourish in the sunlight the way it flourished in the shadows of the night? "What are we going to do?"

"You'll deal with your father," he said.

"And you?"

"I'll wait."

"You will?"

"What else can I do?"

She slid her hands down the damp sleeves of his jacket until her palms met his. He folded his fingers around hers and pulled her to himself. His mouth crushed down on hers; his kiss spoke of hunger and despair, of need and fear. For the first time since she'd raced to her father's side at the foot of the porch steps, she felt her eyes fill with tears.

This was a kiss goodbye.

"Promise me you'll wait."

"I love you, Gillian," he whispered, then abruptly released her, dropped back a step, turned and disappeared into the rainy, moonless night.

Chapter Thirteen

"Why does she not speak with him?" Romeo asked.

Juliet sighed. When first she had brought Owen and Gillian together, she had foreseen that a conflict would arise from his professional background and her family history. Juliet had presumed that her hero and heroine would struggle to find their common ground, their own fertile soil in which to plant the seeds of love. She had known it would not be easy for them.

But this... She had not prepared herself for this.

She gazed dolefully down at the hospital scene below. Strange modern machinery linked to Gillian's father's body issued whirring, beeping noises. Medical practitioners came and went, conversing in low, solemn voices and looking grim.

She had not prepared herself for the violence. Four hundred years after her own impetuous lover had slain her dear cousin Tybalt and Paris, she had hoped that wiser lovers would resolve their disagreements with reason and affection, not unthinking brutality.

"Why did Owen have to assault her father?" she lamented.

Beside her she could feel Romeo quiver with indignation. "Assault her father? He was merely fending off *her father's vicious attack. A man has a right to protect himself.''*

"Men," Juliet groaned. "Everything with men, every quibble and quarrel, must always be decided with fists. Why cannot men sit down and talk things out? Why could not Owen retreat from Sam Chappell's aggression?''

"Retreat! And be taken for a weakling?''

"Alas! This is how men measure their worth. Why can men not see that hurting one another is the wrong way to go about resolving problems?''

"Men are not the only ones who hurt others," Romeo countered. "Your Gillian has hurt Owen.''

"How so? He has nearly killed her father, and yet she loves him still. How does this hurt him?''

"Days have passed since his departure, and she has not spoken to him.''

"How can she? With all she has to attend to—''

"What could be more important than to talk to the man she supposedly loves?''

"The man who gravely wounded her father," Juliet interjected.

Romeo issued a caustic snort of a laugh. "If Gillian truly loved Owen, she would absolve him of any guilt in her father's misfortune. She would contact him.''

"When it is time for Gillian to speak with Owen, she shall speak with him," Juliet insisted. "She thinks of him unceasingly. She dreams of him. But—''

"But in the blackest corner of her soul she believes he is responsible for her father's dire condition. In that abyss of grief, she blames Owen for what has transpired.''

Juliet did not want to believe Romeo, but she lacked the proof to refute him. Perhaps Gillian did blame

Owen. *Perhaps her failure to contact her beloved was due not to circumstances beyond her influence but rather to that abyss Romeo had mentioned, a corrosive suspicion deep within her soul.*

"And if he were truly a man," Romeo went on, "he would not have run. He would have stayed and fought her father again and again."

"He left because he loves her," Juliet argued.

"He should not have run. America is not a monarchy, where a man may be banished by a prince as I was banished from Verona. Sam Chappell is to blame for his own injury. Owen should not be punished."

Juliet understood that Owen's departure was not a punishment. It was a sacrifice, made in love. He had left Verona to give Gillian the opportunity she needed to find forgiveness.

Owen did have to bear part of the blame for what had occurred on a rain-slick porch one week ago. He had pushed Sam Chappell harder than he'd had to. Romeo could justify Owen's actions as self-defense, but Juliet knew better. She knew Owen could have avoided this outcome if he had wished it.

Evidently, he hadn't wished it.

Men were that way, their egos as fragile as Venetian glass, their tempers as volatile as the fire in Etna's forge. The merest threat and they erupted in warfare. They fought with bloodthirsty commitment for their names, their rights, their integrity. They were such fools.

It was a wonder women could love them.

GILLIAN WONDERED HOW she could love Owen.

Despite everything, she still did. And yet, as one day blurred into the next and she watched her father's slow, tortuous journey back to life, she suffered strange mo-

ments, flashes of guilt, twinges of complicity, black
holes of doubt that seemed to suck all her love into a
dense void.

The two most important men in my life, she would
think, staring at her father's pale face, at the flickers of
animation in his eyes, at the motion of his lips and
tongue as he attempted to talk, at the flexing of the fingers of his left hand. *The two most important men in
my life tried to kill each other.*

And Owen had nearly succeeded.

But she loved him. She loved him because he'd been
in the right, because her father had been the one in-
fected with hatred, because Owen was noble enough to
have wanted to turn himself in to the authorities, even
though nothing good would have come of it. She loved
him because she couldn't help herself, because loving
him was a part of her, because without him her life was
unendurable.

Had she sent him away to spare him a pointless encounter with the police? Or to give herself an opportunity to learn how to survive without him, to endure the
unendurable?

"I love him," she told Nancy. They were seated in the
hospital cafeteria, nursing cups of coffee. Perry Royerson had stopped by to sit with her father; Perry had
developed an irksome habit of visiting her father's room
several times a day, even though his business should
have kept him in the pediatrics wing. It was as if he were
trying to make himself indispensable to Gillian.

Nancy stirred a packet of sugar into her coffee. It was
eight o'clock, and Gillian had wanted to spend the last
hour of the evening visiting period with her father. But
Perry had assured her he would keep Sam company
while Gillian took a break from her constant vigil.

"Who do you love? Perry Royerson?" Nancy asked. "He sure has been a darling, hasn't he." She emptied another packet of sugar into her cup and stirred it in with a brown plastic swizzle stick.

"Not Perry. Owen."

Nancy eyed her incredulously. "Owen? The man responsible for all this?"

Gillian considered countering that her father, not Owen, had caused the calamity. But how could she accuse her father of anything when he was lying in a hospital bed, struggling for minutes at a time just to utter the words "yes" and "no?" How could she blame him when he'd lost the battle?

He wasn't the only loser, she reminded herself. She and Owen had lost, too.

"I keep telling myself I shouldn't love him, that it's wrong, it's impossible," she confessed. "But I can't talk myself out of what I'm feeling."

"Maybe you should try," Nancy advised. "What good can come of it? If your father gets better, do you think he'll ever be able to accept Owen? And if, God forbid, he doesn't get better, do you think *you'll* be able to accept Owen, knowing he did this thing?"

Gillian sighed and gazed at her friend. How she wished that life were normal and they were in her house, concocting an exotic Lombardian gourmet feast and guzzling Soave, instead of sitting in this clean, cold, uncomfortable room of glaring lights and folding metal chairs and disagreeing on the most fundamental issue in Gillian's life. She hated the hospital, hated her coffee, hated her father for having attacked Owen.

Hated herself for being unable to stop loving Owen, even with all the black holes of guilt and doubt.

If only she could hate Owen, too, her predicament might be easier. But she couldn't hate him. She could only indulge in those bleak, frightening moments of doubt.

"Have you been in touch with him?"

"I tried to call him once," Gillian said. "He wasn't home."

"Did you leave a message?"

Gillian shook her head. "I heard his machine click on and I hung up. I don't know why. I just...I couldn't bear to hear his voice on a machine. If he were there, if I could have talked to him..." She drifted off, aware that she had no idea what she would have said to him that night if he'd been home. *I love you. I love you, Owen, in spite of everything.*

"Has he called you?"

Gillian shook her head again. She had driven home every night after the visiting hours ended and raced directly to her bedroom to see if her answering machine's message light was flashing. Twice in the past week it was. One call was from her office and the other was from Perry Royerson.

"I think he's trying to give me some space."

"Well isn't that nice? He cracks open your father's skull, and now he wants to give you some space. What a guy."

"Nancy, please." Gillian needed her friend's support, not snide remarks.

"All right." Nancy's tone softened, but her words were harsh. "I'll give him two points for keeping his distance. He knows this grand love affair was wrong from the word go, and he's giving you a chance to get over him. That's the nicest thing he could do for you. And if you've got half the intelligence I give you credit for, you'll put him out of your mind—unless you want to sue him for pain and suffering. It's not my specialty, but I'll file the papers for you if you want."

"I'm not going to sue him, Nancy. For God's sake, I love him!"

Nancy groaned and rolled her eyes. "Get over him, Gillian. The man's brought you nothing but trouble."

No, Gillian wanted to protest. *He's brought me love and passion. He's brought me the ability to see a person for who he is, not who his father was or where he came from. He's brought light into my life. He's soared with me on the wings of night, and together we've tasted heaven.*

There was no way she could explain it to Nancy, who thought the answer to all of life's problems was a playful romp beneath the covers. There was no way Gillian could explain the unexplainable—that love was irrational, that it was joy and pain and everything in between, and that once it had you in its grasp you couldn't escape, not until it was ready to let you go.

"Either forget him," Nancy said, "or make him pay for what he's done."

Gillian lowered her gaze to her coffee. She saw her reflection shivering in the liquid surface, her face washed in the darkness of the drink so she appeared ghostly, wavering, a shadow of herself.

She couldn't forget him. And he'd already paid more than she could measure. So had her father.

So had she.

A WOMAN ANSWERED, "Owen Moore's residence."

Gillian swallowed hard. She knew there were dozens

of innocent reasons why a woman would answer his telephone—she might be his housekeeper, or his sister, or his mother. Or a friend. Just because he'd sworn his love to Gillian didn't mean he couldn't have a female guest at his house.

It had taken so much courage for her to telephone him, though. She had hoped only to hear his voice, to have the husky, loving sound of it counteract all the negative things Nancy had said earlier that evening at the hospital. She needed to know Owen was still with her, still as much in the grip of their love as she was.

"Is Owen there?" she asked, loathing the tenuous sound of her voice.

"No, he had to step out for a few minutes," the woman said. "Can I take a message?"

Gillian wasn't about to ask some strange woman to convey her private, heartfelt, desperate message to Owen. "No," she said quietly. "I'll try again some other time." Before the woman could respond, Gillian hung up.

She stretched out on her bed and stared at the ceiling. Beside her lay the heap of paperwork she'd brought with her from the office. Her father's crisis had thrown her work schedule into a state of upheaval, and although her colleagues had been wonderfully considerate, she couldn't just let all her professional responsibilities slide.

So she worked when she could, late at night and early in the morning. She arose at five, grabbed a quick breakfast, and was at her desk by six, researching, organizing, planning strategies and arguments. By nine, she was in court, and by one she was on the highway, heading to the hospital to spend the afternoon and evening sitting at her father's side, clutching his hand, talking to him, willing him to heal.

By the end of each day, she was drained and distraught. Tonight was no exception. She was upset and frightened, haunted by Nancy's stern admonishment and her own doubts. She lacked the fortitude to say to the strange woman who had answered Owen's phone, "Who the hell are you? Where's the man I love?"

Love should have made her stronger, but it didn't. She felt sapped, battered, excruciatingly lonely. Her father was lying in a hospital room. She was alone in her bed, fully clothed, with a stack of file folders for company.

And the man she loved, the man responsible for her father's horrible situation, was three thousand miles away in Venice, California.

With another woman.

OWEN KICKED THE DOOR SHUT behind him and carried his paper sack into the kitchen. He pulled out the bottle, yanked a glass from a cupboard and poured in an inch of scotch.

Rosalie wandered in from the deck. "Did you get what you needed?"

What Owen needed wasn't for sale in a liquor store. What he needed was in Verona, but he couldn't have it. Not until she called. *If* she called.

He took a belt of the whiskey, then nudged the bottle toward her and nodded. "Do you want some?"

"No thanks. We're enjoying the wine." She and her husband had brought a bottle of Chardonnay with them when they'd come for dinner. But Owen needed something stronger than wine. Something stronger, even, than scotch, although it would have to do.

Rosalie watched as he methodically rolled up the sleeves of his shirt and pulled a platter of steak from the refrigerator. Through the glass sliding door, he signaled Rosalie's husband to turn on the gas grill.

He wasn't sure why he'd invited them over. Probably because after his meeting with Ben Voltz earlier that day, he'd known he would do something stupid if he were alone that night, like fly back to New Jersey, or drink himself into oblivion.

He might still drink himself into oblivion, he thought, taking another sip from his glass. But in front of witnesses, he'd have to do it slower.

That afternoon, Ben had swept into Owen's office, beaming. "Great news," he'd said. "I just got word from Harvey Shoup."

"What news?"

"Our troublemaker at Sandifer Chemicals can't make trouble anymore."

Had Sam died? "What do you mean?" Owen asked quietly.

"Sam Chappell. The firebrand shop steward. He fell down and broke his crown, just like in the nursery rhyme."

"How is he?" Owen's voice had been calm, his face impassive, his nervous system going haywire. "Will he live?"

"Apparently. But he won't be returning to work any time soon. Maybe never. It's a head injury, Owen. Who knows how much he'll get back?"

"I want him to have the best of everything," Owen had said, laboring to present himself as nothing more than a concerned, compassionate executive. "If he needs supplemental health insurance, put it through.

Living expenses, disability pension—whatever he needs."

"Owen. I'm beginning to think you're the one with the head injury. We've finally rid ourselves of a troublemaker—"

"*Rid ourselves?* Are you implying that *we* had anything to do with this accident?" After spiriting him away so he wouldn't be held accountable, had Gillian decided to go public with the truth surrounding her father's fall? Had she come to believe Owen had pushed Sam down the steps in order to eliminate a troublesome union man from his firm's newest acquisition?

"Apparently the only person with him when he fell was his daughter, the labor lawyer. Heaven knows, maybe she was tired of his stubborn-fool approach to labor issues—"

"She adores her father," Owen had snapped. "She would never do anything to hurt him."

"Then it was simply luck," Ben had concluded. "Bad luck for the Chappells and good luck for us. Drink a toast to yourself, Owen. Purchasing Sandifer Chemicals might have just turned into a stroke of genius."

He'd wanted to drink a toast to himself, all right. Several toasts, enough toasts to numb the pain eating at his gut, at his soul. Instead, he'd called Rosalie and invited her and her husband to join him for dinner. It was an act of self-preservation, nothing more.

"Someone phoned while you were out," Rosalie reported, then pursed her lips in disapproval as Owen drained his glass and refilled it.

"Who?"

"I don't know. She wouldn't say."

She.

He set the bottle down with a dull thud, avoiding Rosalie's curious gaze. Please, he thought, please let it be Gillian.

"Did she leave a message?" he asked.

"No."

"Is she going to call back?"

"She said she would."

He filled his lungs with air and let it out slowly. Whoever she was, she would call again.

Gillian would call. She would reach out to him in his exile and assure him that in spite of everything, her love for him hadn't died.

He had lost track of the number of times he'd lifted the phone to call her, but he'd always hung up before he'd finished dialing. He couldn't initiate the contact. She might not be ready for him. If her father's condition hadn't improved, if she couldn't bring herself to forgive Owen, if she ultimately decided that family loyalty was more important than love . . .

He couldn't call her. He had to give her the time she needed to listen to her own heart and decide.

And if she decided to cut him from her life?

He would hate her father for having torn them apart. And hate her for having lost faith in their love. And hate himself for having cared so much, having fallen for her, having touched an enchanted statue in Italy. He would drink a lot of scotch and hate everyone who crossed his path.

Maybe it wouldn't come to that. Gillian had told him she loved him, with her words, with her body, with the passion of her lips on his, her hands on him, her warmth opening to him and drawing him in and making him a part of her. She had told him with her pulse and her breath, with her cascading golden brown hair and her magnificent green eyes. She had told him freely, honestly, jubilantly.

He wanted to believe that was enough.

"The grill's ready," Rosalie's husband called through the screen door.

Owen nodded and seasoned the steak with tenderizer. "I'll be the chef tonight," Rosalie offered, reaching around him to lift the platter. "While I cook, you can tell us all about New Jersey."

"New Jersey," he echoed. *Verona.* The real Verona, the only Verona that counted, the Verona that bewitched him, that was home to the most bewitching woman in the world.

The Verona where he wanted to be, with her, forever. The Verona where he couldn't be, not until she forgave him. Not until she told him their love could overcome anything.

Even reality.

With a desolate sigh, he picked up his glass and followed Rosalie out of the kitchen.

BY THE SECOND WEEK, the hospital staff was beginning to use the word "miracle" in reference to her father. He had progressed from the very brink of death to consciousness, to controlled movement, to sitting, to squeezing Gillian's hand, to the beginnings of slow, faltering speech.

Everyone who worked with him told Gillian that he was most responsive when she was with him. So she spent as much time at his side as she could. Juggling her files and her laptop computer, she would accompany him to the physical-therapy room and sit on the side, plowing through her own work while the therapists exercised his arms and legs. She would push his wheelchair for him, read the newspaper to him, comb his hair and cut his meat. She would stay in his room until the nurse shooed her out at nine o'clock. Then she would go to her father's house and rearrange furniture in preparation for his eventual return home. Some nights she would be too exhausted to drive back to Verona, and she would trudge up the stairs to her old childhood bedroom for the night.

One evening, while she was taking her father for an after-dinner airing in the hospital's courtyard garden, he said, "Insurance."

"What?"

"Insurance." He craned his head to peer up at her from his wheelchair. He looked worried. "Medical insurance?"

"You're covered," she said.

"I am?"

"Not only do you have complete medical coverage, but you're receiving a disability pension."

"I am?"

She was pleased to see the sparkle of surprise in his green eyes. Last week they'd looked foggy to her, but today they looked clear and bright. "You are," she said. "Moore Enterprises has an excellent pension plan. If you can go back to work—and the way you're improving, there's a good chance of that—then you're covered for as long as you're out. If you can't go back to work, they'll pay for any extra training you need if you want to qualify for another job. Or they'll continue your disability."

"How long?"

"For the rest of your life."

His eyes grew wider. He shook his head. Gillian ought to have been impressed by how well he was communicating, but all she could think of was Owen. The policies her father was so afraid of—the policies that had driven him to assail Owen—were saving his life and safeguarding his future.

"Sit," her father said.

She pushed the wheelchair over to a bench, turned it so her father would be able to see her and then obediently took a seat.

"I'm getting better," he said.

"Yes. Of course you are. The doctors say—"

"Not my head." Moving arduously, he raised his right hand to his heart, as if about to recite the pledge of allegiance. "Here. It's getting better."

"There was no heart damage, Dad."

"But there was room for improvement." Aware of how difficult it was for him to string so many words together, she wanted to reassure him that he didn't have to say anything more. But he seemed to think he *did* have to say these things, so she smothered her protective impulses and waited patiently for his next statement.

"I was a fool."

"You tripped, Dad. It was an accident."

"I was a fool." He exhaled. "Owen."

She bit her lip and blinked away the tears that suddenly blurred her vision of the lawns, the lush foliage of the shade trees, the pink-hued dusk sky. "What about Owen?" she managed.

"To hate him. A waste."

"Don't punish yourself, Dad—"

"Already punished," he said with a wry smile and a wave toward the oversize wheels of his chair. He flexed his mouth, struggling to shape the words. His voice was weak but steady. "You love him?"

"Yes."

"Then go."

"Dad. You need me here. The doctors say—"

He shook his head. "Lettie and Charlie. I'll be okay." He extended his quivering hand to her. "Go. Listen to your heart and go."

Her heart had been urging her to go to Owen. Ever since that afternoon in a courtyard in Verona, Italy, it had been singing one song, whispering one secret, urging one goal: *Go to him.*

"I love you, Dad," she murmured, feeling a few tears leak through her lashes and skitter down her cheeks.

"I love you, too. Go. Tell him I'm sorry." A tear slid down his weathered cheek. "I hope it's not too late."

Within an hour she was in her bedroom, dialing his number, listening to the phone ring and ring. And ring.

He wasn't home.

That was all right. She would leave a message. She would tell him that nothing stood between them any more, not hatred, not resentment, not family prejudices, not historical animosities. She would tell Owen that she loved him, that she could not recall a single moment in the past two weeks—in the past two years— when he hadn't been in her thoughts. She would tell him that she would leave Verona and come to him, free to love him.

His answering machine didn't click on. The phone rang twenty times, and she hung up.

It shouldn't have disturbed her. People had the right to turn off their answering machines whenever they wanted. But now, when her long, miserable ordeal was over, she needed to hear Owen's voice—even if only on a tape. She needed to touch him in some way, to let him know that the clouds were beginning to part and the first rays of light were peeking through.

She abandoned her bed for her desk. In the middle drawer, she found a sheet of stationery. *Dear Owen,* she began. *I love you.* That was all she had to say right now, the most important thing. The rest could wait until she was in his arms. She signed her name, folded the letter, stuffed it into an envelope, and dug the address of Moore Enterprises from the sheaf of employee information he'd given her the first time she'd seen him at Sandifer Chemicals. She didn't have his home address.

She got ready for bed, folded back the blankets and tried him on the telephone once more. No answer.

Dear Owen, I love you, she sighed, as if the words could ward off the apprehension that nibbled at her. When she'd left her father she'd felt so hopeful, so full of faith that the future would belong to Owen and her, that at long last she had the answer to *What are we going to do?* They were going to love each other. They were going to be together. They were going to build a life together.

But he was out of reach. She could write, she could keep trying him on the telephone, but what if she couldn't get to him?

What am I going to do? she wondered, staring up into the darkness and trying to hold her anxiety at bay.

She was going to keep trying. Keep hoping. Keep loving him.

She had no choice.

HE ARRIVED HOME late, after a long walk on the boardwalk. He'd watched the water surge and retreat, watched the moon tiptoe across the waves. He'd counted the days since he'd left Gillian and realized that the number was too great.

She hadn't forgiven him.

He had spoken to John Balthasar at Sandifer Chemicals earlier that day. The manager had reported that Sam Chappell still had a long convalescence ahead of him. "What a freaky thing," John had remarked. "Sam Chappell was as strong as a bull, you know? Strong and fit and athletic. Every year at the company picnic softball game he'd taken the slugger title. It's hard to believe he could just trip and fall like that."

He hadn't just tripped and fallen. Owen had pushed him.

If he loved her less he would call her and pressure her. He would demand that she quit hiding and say what she had to say to him: *I hate you. You've ruined my father's life and mine.*

He entered his house, locked the door behind him, and wandered through the dark rooms to his bedroom. His body ached with a loneliness to match his soul. He needed her.

And she hadn't forgiven him. Obviously she couldn't.

He lifted his telephone, started to dial her number as he had a zillion times in the past two weeks, and then thought better of it. Returning to the kitchen, he rummaged through his briefcase until he found the slip of paper with Nancy Burdette's home phone number on it. He punched the long-distance number into the buttons, listened to the phone ring a few times, and then she answered, sounding breathless and dazed. "H'lo?"

"Nancy? This is Owen Moore."

A silence, and then, "Do you know what time it is?"

Eleven-fifteen, California time. Three hours later in New York. "I'm sorry. Did I wake you?"

"Actually...no. I was...busy."

Great. He'd interrupted her in the midst of something no doubt torrid and intimate and wonderful, something Owen would have liked to be doing with Gillian right now. "I'm sorry."

"Yeah, well...um...could we make this quick?"

"I need to know how Gillian is."

"She hasn't called you?"

"No. Unless she might have tried tonight. My sister's in town for a few days and she filched my answering machine. But there haven't been any messages before now, and... Damn it, Nancy—I need to know. How is she?"

"How do you think she is?" Nancy snapped. "Juggling her work and spending every minute she can with her father. She's in a state of chronic exhaustion."

His heart pounded erratically; he heard the drumbeat in his skull and felt it in the pit of his stomach.

"I haven't seen her in over a week," Nancy continued. "I talked to her a couple of days ago and she said she was running on empty, she hadn't gotten a good night's sleep in ages. She's a wreck, Owen. An absolute wreck."

He cursed. He had no reason to doubt Nancy; she was Gillian's best friend. If Gillian was a wreck, he was the one who had wrecked her.

"I suppose if she wanted to talk to you she would have called you by now," Nancy added.

His pulse grew louder, slower, banging time to a funeral march. "Well. Thanks."

"Yeah. Stay away from her, Owen, okay? The only way she's going to get through this is if you stay out of her life."

He lowered the phone into its cradle and closed his eyes.

Stay out of her life. Nancy's final words hovered in his skull, a bitter counterpoint to the beating of his heart. Gillian couldn't deal with him. She was a wreck. *If she wanted to talk to you she would have called you by now.*

If she hadn't forgiven him by now, she never would.

It's over, he conceded. It's over. He would never stop loving her, and she would never forgive him, and it was over.

The house was still, silent as death. He turned off the light and let the dark, humid night close around him.

Chapter Fourteen

The train from Milan pulled into the Verona station with a squeak of brakes and a hiss of steam. Gillian was beyond tired; jet lag, emotional fatigue and the sultry Mediterranean heat hung around her like a velvet drape, heavy and smothering.

She dragged her suitcase down the steps to the platform. Across the broad boulevard, through the summer haze, she could see the elegant modern edifice of the Hotel Leon D'Oro.

She wasn't staying there this time. Her budget couldn't accommodate the airfare to Italy, let alone a room in the most elegant hotel in Verona. Her father, of all people, had insisted on paying for her plane ticket. "You've been so good to me," he'd said. "I can spare it. Hey, I won't be taking any vacation trips for a while."

Actually, he could take a vacation if he wanted. He was already on his feet—he relied on a walker for balance, and climbing the stairs was still beyond his ability, but he was getting around. Uncle Charlie had taken him fishing a few times, and Aunt Lettie and the day nurse paid for by Sandifer's generous insurance were keeping her father well fed, well groomed and well along the path to recovery.

"Go," he'd ordered Gillian. "You need to get away."

No argument there. She needed to get as far away as she could from her life, from her grief, from the agony of knowing that just when happiness had seemed to be within her reach, she'd lost Owen.

She didn't understand it. She'd phoned him again and again. She'd gotten his answering machine, left message after message, then phoned and heard a series of beeps that indicated the message tape was full, then phoned and heard no machine at all.

She'd mailed him the letter in which she'd written that she loved him. And the next day, in another, more lucid letter she had described her father's progress and requested that Owen call her so they could talk. She'd sent yet another one a week later, saying, "Just give me a sign. If you want me to leave you alone, Owen, I will, but you've got to let me know."

She'd heard nothing.

Finally she'd telephoned his office. When she'd requested Owen Moore, the receptionist had routed her call to someone named Ben Voltz. "I'm the acting president of Moore Enterprises," he'd said. "What can I do for you?"

She'd frowned, puzzled by his title. "This is Gillian Chappell. I'd like to speak to Owen, please."

"Ah. Ms. Chappell. The labor lawyer."

"I'm calling on a personal—"

"I understand your father is recuperating, Ms. Chappell. John Balthasar of Sandifer Chemicals keeps us apprised. Should we be preparing for your father's return to Sandifer? Because, believe me, if he's planning to return, we want to be prepared for him."

"I didn't call on business, Mr. Voltz," she'd said brusquely. "I need to speak to Owen. It's personal."

"Owen Moore doesn't want to speak to you," he'd responded.

The words were like a dagger between the ribs, turning, twisting, draining her of her life. "Did he tell you to say that?" she'd asked, barely able to keep the shock and pain out of her voice.

"Owen doesn't want to speak to anyone, Ms. Chappell. He's taken a leave of absence."

"A leave of absence?"

"That's right. He's closed up his house and put me in charge here. He's gone."

"Gone? Gone where?"

"I have no idea."

She'd waited for Ben to elaborate. When he hadn't, she'd asked, "Is there any way at all that I can reach him?"

"He doesn't want to be reached, Ms. Chappell. He's left no forwarding address. So you may as well stop sending him letters, too. He obviously doesn't want to be bothered."

Fine. She wouldn't bother him. She would vanish, just as he had vanished. She would get away, as her father had urged her. She would go somewhere to lick her wounds, to regroup her strength, to try to mend her heart the way her father had mended his head. She would go somewhere by herself and figure out a way to survive the next sixty years without Owen.

She lugged her suitcase down the stairs to the parking lot. A cab cruised over to the curb and the driver peered hopefully at her through the window.

She flipped through her phrase book. *"Per favore, mi vuol portare all'albergo Fabiano,"* she said, her pronunciation as uncertain as her father's had been when he'd been trying to relearn how to speak.

"*Albergo* Fabiano?" the driver repeated, then threw back his head and guffawed. "*Sì, sì.*" He reached behind him and opened the rear door for her. "*Ti porto.*"

She wasn't sure what was so hilarious about her having asked him to take her to the Fabiano Hotel. Maybe her accent was funny. And she probably looked wretched, her hair leaking out of the barrette into which she'd clipped it, her clothing wrinkled from the transatlantic flight and the two-hour train trip.

Let him laugh at her. She didn't care. She just wanted to get to the hotel and lie down.

When he coasted to a halt at a narrow door in a narrow alley, she realized why he'd laughed. The sign posted outside the second-floor window was so badly weather-beaten it was scarcely readable. The shutters hung crookedly against the eroded stucco wall; the granite steps leading to the front door were crumbled and listing. To call the Fabiano a hotel was overstating things by a bit.

However, it cost a hell of a lot less than the Leon D'Oro.

She paid the driver, dragged her suitcase out of the car and ascended the lopsided steps to the door. She entered a claustrophobically gloomy hallway furnished with a couple of lumpy-looking chairs and a marble-topped table. A tiny, white-haired woman bounded through an inner door.

"*Per favore,*" Gillian began, remembering with nostalgia how well the staff at the Hotel Leon D'Oro spoke English. "My name is Gillian Chappell—"

"Ah! Signorina Chappell!"

Signora Fabiano prattled in bubbly Italian as she led Gillian up two rickety flights of stairs to a third-floor room overlooking the alley. The room had a bed, a sink, a nightstand and a threadbare rug. Gillian didn't suppose she needed anything more. She thanked Signora Fabiano and mumbled, in her awkward Italian, that she wanted to rest.

Alone in the tiny room, she closed the door and crossed to the open window. The wall of the building across the way was dark brown stone, with an undisciplined rose vine climbing the wall. The flowers were in full bloom, a vivid, cloying red.

Gillian remembered another red rose, another place, a time when she'd believed that love was the solution to all difficulties, not the source of them.

Why had she come to Verona? It was only going to make the pain worse.

She was here because she had to come, had to work through the pain. Had to exorcise Owen from her soul. She was here because she had to confront that infernal statue of Juliet—and knock it off its pedestal, if that was what it took to break the spell.

Tears streamed down her face, and she let them. She no longer had put on a show of good cheer for her father or her other relatives or her colleagues at work. She could inhale the voluptuous scent of the roses in the alley and weep until she had no tears left inside her. Crying made her feel weak, but so what? She was in Italy now, far from her family, her job, the bed she'd shared with Owen, the wondrous love she'd shared with him. She could be weak.

She stumbled across the tiny room to the bed and flopped across it. Her mind drifted; she lapsed in and out of slumber, in and out of dreams. Dreams of Owen holding her, caressing her skin, gazing down at her with eyes as dark as infinity yet bright with passion, with reverence. Owen kissing her, becoming a part of her, redefining her body, her mind, her understanding of desire.

When she woke up, she was disoriented. The light in the room had shifted, sending long stripes of shadow across her bed. Her watch told her it was mid-afternoon; her inner clock told her early morning.

She yawned, stretched, and tried to ignore the cricks and cramps left by the airplane and the train. Her short nap had restored her energy. She unpacked her bag, brushed out the snarls in her hair, and headed down the teetering stairs and out of the hotel.

The scent of roses wrapped around her. She broke into a run, as if by escaping the alley she could escape the fragrance and all the memories it evoked.

Clutching her street map and her phrase book, she stalked down one side street and another until she reached the *Corso Porto Nuova*. Looming in the distance were the towering stone arches of the Arena.

She kept her gaze focused on the cobblestone sidewalk in front of her as she neared the amphitheater where she and Owen had first spoken, first kissed. She moved at a brisk pace, concentrating on the chore of placing one foot and then the other before her until she was safely past the ancient monument. Then another block, another picturesque, vaguely familiar street of stone houses with wooden shutters, of olive and cottonwood trees and vining roses. Through an archway, up another alley and into the courtyard.

It looked exactly as she'd remembered it: the ivy-covered brick walls, the carved balcony, the Gothic windows, the wooden benches, the statue of Juliet, tarnished except for her shiny arm and breast, and the wishful tourists, yammering in a multitude of languages but all of them saying the same thing with their smiles as they embraced the statue: *Bring me love! Give me luck in love!*

Gillian threaded her way past the tourists with their cameras and their fantasies. She marched up to the statue and reached out her hand. But just as she'd been unable to keep from touching it last time, this time she couldn't seem to place her fingers against the bronze. It was as if the statue had an aura, a force field that prevented Gillian from touching it.

You had that chance, Juliet seemed to be saying. *You had your love.*

And I lost him, Gillian wanted to scream. Our love was put to too great a test. My love could have overcome the obstacles, but Owen's couldn't.

I don't want another chance, Gillian wanted to tell the statue. I don't ever want to fall in love again. I just want my sanity back.

That she was standing in front of a sculpted figure of metal, silently pleading with it, was proof enough that she was far from sane.

Sighing brokenly, Gillian turned away. How far she'd come since the day two years ago when she'd laughed at the idea that a statue could perform magic. Yet as far as she'd come, look where she'd wound up: exactly where she'd started. A believer this time. Fortune's fool.

She walked back to the hotel in the sticky afternoon heat. Sweat gathered at the nape of her neck and created a halo of frizz out of her hair. Her camp shirt fell limp around her body; needles of pain pricked her eyes. Why had she returned to Verona? How could she have expected the statue to make everything better? It was only a lump of bronze, nothing more.

Signora Fabiano and several other people—the hotel's other guests, Gillian presumed—were seated in the musty high-ceilinged parlor off the entry, sipping wine and tea and chattering gaily in Italian. Gillian was in no mood to be sociable. She tried to sneak past the doorway and up the stairs to her room.

She didn't make it. "Ah, Signorina Chappell!" Signora Fabiano cried out, hurrying to the doorway and hooking her hand through the bend in Gillian's elbow. Dragging Gillian into the parlor, she beamed at the others. "We have with us American!"

"American! *Buon giorno! Molto lieta!*"

Gillian felt herself being nudged into a chair. Its upholstery was too soft, and she sank deep into the cushions, as if they were sponges sucking her in. A stocky older man in baggy beige trousers and a tweed blazer settled into a chair near her and handed her a glass of wine. "I speak little bit English," he said, smiling gently.

Gillian stared at him. His hair was silver, stretching in distinct strands over the nearly bald crown of his head. Although his shirt was open at the collar, his wool blazer should have overheated him, but she saw no hint that he was at all uncomfortable in the stuffy room.

She managed a feeble smile. *"Buon giorno,"* she said, then took a sip of the crisp, dry wine.

"You visit Verona for some reason?"

Oh, yes—to scream at a statue. "I've been here before," she answered, clinging to her goblet as she settled deeper and deeper into the plush brocade cushions.

"And you come back!" He translated what she'd said to the half dozen other people in the room, then turned back to her. "So. You know about our Giulietta."

"The statue, you mean? Yes, I know." *Too well*, she almost added.

"She brings the good luck."

"She brought me bad luck," Gillian retorted. She immediately regretted her cross tone. The elderly man looked stricken, then deeply concerned. When he translated her statement to the others, a low hum of worried commentary ensued.

"You have a bad luck with your lover?"

Oh, God, how had she gotten drawn into this conversation? She didn't want to discuss her heartache with a group of strangers in a down-at-the-heels *pensione*.

She drank her wine, eyeing the solemn, commiserating guests hovering around her. They meant well. And surely she'd do no worse talking about her sad love affair with these people than she had talking about it with Nancy, who had advised her to forget about Owen. As if such a thing were possible.

"*Sì,*" she replied. "Yes. I've had bad luck with him."

Another swell of voices, murmuring compassionately. A woman suggested something, her voice high and musical but her meaning incomprehensible to Gillian. Signora Fabiano stepped forward, nodding vigorously. "*Sì, sì!*" she said before launching into a lively discourse.

The man in the tweed blazer bowed toward Gillian. "They say," he explained, "you must go seek help at La Tomba."

"La Tomba?"

"Tomba della Giulietta. Juliet's tomb."

"Her *tomb?*" Gillian was in a wretched enough state from her close encounter with Juliet's statue. She wasn't about to go looking for trouble at Juliet's tomb.

"*Sì*. Is a tomb where . . . what is word? The lovelorn. You write letter to Giulietta and leave it at La Tomba, and if you are lucky Giulietta will respond. She give advice how to fix."

Two years ago, Gillian would have laughed out loud. The idea of using the tomb of a Shakespearean character as a mailbox to communicate with some sort of make-believe Dear Abby would have stricken her as absolutely absurd.

But two years ago, Gillian hadn't known what strange magic this city and its most celebrated heroine were capable of.

She knew now, and she didn't laugh. "Where is this tomb?"

"No, no, no!" the woman with the musical voice cried out, while Signora Fabiano began rattling off instructions.

"They say, *primo*—first, you write letter."

"Oh."

Signora Fabiano thrust a pen and a sheet of paper at her. *"Me lo scriva,"* she commanded.

"She says, write it down. Your plea to Giulietta. Maybe you be lucky and she will help."

Gillian wasn't about to trust her luck. And the idea of putting her anguish into words in front of all these strangers, even if only one of them would be able to read what she wrote, embarrassed her. Yet she couldn't let her audience down. They all looked so anxious, so sympathetic.

So, feeling like an idiot, she wrote. She wrote about how her father had tried to keep her from her lover.

About how her lover had accidentally hurt her father, nearly killing him. About how her father had recovered, had seen how wrong he'd been—and how by then it was too late, her lover had disappeared. She wrote that Juliet had brought her and Owen together in the first place, and that if she didn't bring them back together again, Juliet would bear responsibility for Gillian's lifelong misery, because Gillian still loved Owen and would love him forever.

It was an impassioned letter, not one of the cool, businesslike missives she might write in her role as a lawyer or the chatty, newsy notes she might send to her friends. This was a letter that spilled from her heart. She held nothing back.

Fortunately, the silver-haired man didn't ask to read it. He handed Gillian an envelope, and she quickly folded and sealed the letter.

"Buono," someone called out, and *"Adesso! Tu vai!"*

"That means," the elderly man told her, "you go now. Bring your note. May Giulietta guide you."

Signora Fabiano took Gillian's Verona map and marked a huge *X* where the tomb was located. *"Buona fortuna!"* several people shouted, and then she was on her way.

It was a long walk, but the heat didn't feel quite so oppressive. The sun was lower in the sky, the humidity waning. As many times as Gillian told herself that this was a fool's errand, she felt a little better. Maybe the wine she'd drunk had taken effect.

She'd walked nearly a half hour before she finally came upon an old chapel. She stepped into a central courtyard surrounded by a cloistered walkway. The garden was roped off, forcing her toward a gate where she was asked to fork over five thousand lire.

She entered a small museum filled with mediocre Renaissance paintings. She hurried through it, up some stairs to the second floor, past more mediocre paintings and sculptures and down some stairs into a large hall with a large mediocre painting.

If this tomb was so magical, why couldn't Juliet have decorated the place with better artwork? Gillian wondered cynically.

She left the large hall and found herself in the courtyard. Under other circumstances, she might have lingered in the pretty gardens, strolling up and down the walkways and admiring the plantings. But she was on a mission—an insane one. She just wanted to get it over with and then return to the hotel and polish off a few more glasses of wine.

On one side of the courtyard, she spotted a short stairway leading down. She descended and entered a corridor barely lit by the tiny windows set high into the cool stone walls. She followed a winding corridor into an empty room, through it and around a bend.

The chamber she came to was occupied by a cold, heavy casket carved from a single block of granite. It must have been at least seven feet long and four feet wide—much too big for the dainty fourteen-year-old who was supposed to be interred in it. A huge chunk of stone had been chipped from one corner.

Gillian approached the sarcophagus cautiously, passing in and out of the squares of light from the high windows. A modest-size crowd of tourists circled the casket, murmuring, snapping photos, clutching envelopes and squares of notepaper. Closer yet, Gillian realized that the sarcophagus had no lid.

She took a deep breath and peered in, almost afraid she was going to come face to face with Juliet's corpse. The massive casket was filled with letters. Dozens of them. Hundreds.

Dear God, she thought. So many sad people, so much heartbreak in the world. So many people like her, desperate enough to journey to Verona just to participate in this ridiculous charade.

Well, she'd come this far. She might as well go the rest of the way.

Taking a deep breath, she closed her eyes and tossed in her note.

Behind her she heard the shuffling of feet as a swarm of tourists left the room, whispering among themselves. She kept her eyes shut, not wanting to see if they were laughing at her, pointing to her and murmuring, "What a loser! She must be crazy to buy into this goofy myth!"

Eventually the shuffling and hushed voices faded into silence. Taking another long, bracing breath, she opened her eyes.

There, on the opposite side of the sarcophagus, stood a man. Staring at her.

Owen.

HE'D SPENT OVER A week in Venice, but it had done no good.

He'd thought the visual splendor, the canals, the *palazzi*, the bridges and churches and pigeons and gondolas would soothe his bruised psyche. But for some reason, unrelated to the scenic beauty of the city, all he could think of was his own Venice, California, where he'd spent weeks waiting for Gillian to forgive him.

She hadn't.

Of course she hadn't. He had demolished her family. How could she possibly find a place for him in her heart?

He didn't blame her, but still... he had hoped.

Just that morning he had taken the train to Verona. He'd realized being there was only going to hurt even more, but he'd figured it was time to toughen up. He had to inure himself to the pain, build up a resistance to it. He had to get used to being alone, and what better place to begin his training than in a city synonymous with love?

His old landlady from two years ago was delighted to hear from him. She couldn't give him the flat he and Rosalie had rented—it was currently occupied—but she had a nice little room off the kitchen where he was welcome to stay for only eighty thousand lire a night. He took it.

Roaming the familiar streets of Verona, he recalled little of the ten months he'd spent there. Every memory of the place seemed encapsulated into the sixteen hours when he'd known Gillian was sharing Verona with him. That bookstore—he'd walked past it after placing Gillian in a cab. That fruit stand—he'd passed it on his way to *12 Apostoli*, the restaurant where he'd learned her name from her credit card. The Arena...

The circular stone amphitheater loomed before him like an enemy's fort. It was there that the statue's spell had first manifested itself. He remembered chasing after Gillian, searching for her in the winding, curving passageways, darting in and out of the shadows and suddenly seeing her, touching her, knowing that, for every reason and no reason at all, she was the woman he loved.

If he were a more violent man, he would buy some explosives and blow the damned building to smithereens.

He hurried past it, anxious to reach the statue. Perhaps if he blew *that* up, he would spare a few more fortunate souls the bitterness he was experiencing now.

But the courtyard was full of people. Happy, hopeful people. Why should he contaminate the scene with his anger?

There was another place he could go. He remembered hearing about it two years ago, chuckling when people claimed that the spirit of Juliet could help starcrossed lovers there: *La Tomba*.

He wasn't chuckling any more.

He returned to the bookshop and purchased a pad and pencil. He scribbled his note across it, folded it, and asked the clerk for a strip of tape to seal it. So what if this was a pointless exercise, a stupid waste of time and money? He had nothing more to lose, not pride, not hope, not love.

An organized group of Swiss tourists was entering the tomb when he arrived, and as soon as he'd paid the entry fee he joined them. It made him feel less idiotic to be in a crowd, even though he understood only a third of what they said in their oddly accented French. Together with them he ambled through the first few rooms, pretending to be interested in the trite paintings and second-rate statues that cluttered the museum, pretending to be impressed by the charming little garden at the center of the building.

He stayed with them as they trooped down the short stairway and into the mausoleum. Their voices bounced off the chilly stone walls; their footsteps echoed on the hard floors as they turned the corner and entered what was alleged to have been Juliet's final resting place.

The Swiss tourists posed, took pictures, laughed and tossed letters into the sarcophagus. Owen drifted away from them and stood back against the wall, no longer eager to be in their boisterous, jovial company. If he were his old rational self, he would have laughed along with them at the preposterousness of dropping love notes into an open granite coffin. This was a lark, a joke, something truly silly.

But he didn't feel silly. He felt like a man who had never really known what love was until he'd met Gillian. Until he'd kissed her and held her and talked to her, and discovered that three thousand miles and wildly differing backgrounds were irrelevant. Until he'd realized that he loved her so much he would force himself to stay away from her.

As the throng of Swiss tourists began to drift toward the exit, he stepped forward, dropped his note into the casket—and saw Gillian standing on the other side of the room.

She wore a white blouse and pale skirt that displayed the golden undertone of her complexion. Her hair was a marvel of untamed waves shimmering down her back. Her eyes were closed, her lower lip caught in her teeth, her hands clenched before her, either in prayer or in pain.

At first he thought he was hallucinating. How could she be here? She was in New Jersey, taking care of her father, locking Owen out of her life.

But then she opened her eyes. They were moss green, the most beautiful eyes he'd ever seen, and they were brimming with anguish.

He knew he wasn't hallucinating.

She gazed at him from across the imposing block of granite that stood between them. Had it actually been Juliet's tomb at one time? Had the world's most romantic heroine once lain dead in this place, surrounded by the bodies of her cousin, her fiancé and her one true love, her Romeo? To walk around the casket would be like tramping across their graves.

Owen would hike through hell to be with Gillian. He circled the casket and took her hands in his.

She gazed at him, looking at first stunned by his presence and then resigned. Like him, she was probably thinking this was just one more bit of inexplicable magic, one more event over which they had no control, one more element of proof that destiny was running the show.

"What did you write in your letter?" she asked.

With anyone else he would have been abashed at having been caught throwing a note into a tomb. But Gillian understood; she'd thrown in a note herself.

He slid his thumbs back and forth along her knuckles, savoring her smooth velvet skin, relishing the feel of her, her nearness and warmth. "I wrote," he confessed, "that I love a woman, but I've caused her pain."

"Owen—"

"I wrote that I can't stand knowing how much damage I've done to her, and I can't stand knowing I'll never have her in my arms again." He stared at her hands enveloped in his. It would be so easy to slide his hands up her arms and around her, to gather her to himself and cover her lips with his.

It would be the most difficult thing in the world.

"What did you write?" he asked.

"That I tried and tried to reach the man I love, that I telephoned and wrote him letters—"

"I never got any letters!"

"But he went away. He left me. And there was no way I could tell him I love him."

Owen's heart stopped beating for a minute, then began again, strong and vigorous, almost hurting from happiness. "You can tell him now."

"I love you," she whispered, her glorious green eyes unwavering, her hands curling anxiously around his.

"I love you," he murmured, bringing his arms around her at last and crushing his mouth to hers.

After an endless minute, Gillian broke from him. Her eyes were still unwavering, still shimmering with unspoken emotion. "What are we going to do?" she asked.

She sounded helpless, as she always did when they faced that impossible question. But it no longer seemed impossible to him. It *was* in his control, after all. He had choices. He had his love, he had Gillian, and he could do whatever he wanted.

"I'll live with you in Verona," he said. "Venice isn't our place. Verona is."

"But your job—"

"I'll set up shop in New York. I've got legal and financial people there. We'll make it work, Gillian. I'll make peace with your father, if he'll let me."

"My father will make peace with you," she assured him. "Sometimes it takes a knock on the head to make a person see things in a new way. It's my father's doing that we're together here. He paid for me to come to Italy."

"He had no way of knowing I'd be here."

"But if he hadn't paid the airfare, I might not have been able to come. Forgive him, Owen, because he's forgiven you. He may disagree with you about everything in the world. But he knows I love you, and that's the most important thing.''

''You'll have to meet my family, too.'' Owen ran his fingers through her luxuriant hair, over her strong, lovely shoulders, down the sleek slope of her back. ''You'll disagree with them about everything—and it won't matter.''

''Nothing matters but this.'' She leaned into his kiss as he bowed to her. Unlike their last kiss, this one was slow, deep, not an explosion but a confirmation, a commitment, an eternal promise.

The distant, distorted sound of voices informed them of the approach of another group of tourists. Gillian and Owen separated and smiled into each other's eyes. ''We should pull out our letters,'' Gillian said, turning toward the sarcophagus. ''We don't need Juliet's help any more.''

''To tell you the truth,'' Owen muttered, slipping his arm around Gillian's waist as they bellied up to the granite casket, ''I'd just as soon Juliet stayed out of our lives from now on.''

Gillian's fingers tensed over the rim of the casket. Her eyes grew round, darting back and forth. ''It's gone!''

''Your note?''

''It should be right here. It was a stiff envelope, with *Albergo Fabiano* printed on it. It's gone!''

''So is mine,'' he said with a frown as he searched the piles of notes on the far side of the casket. He'd noticed that his was the only letter that hadn't been sealed into an envelope. The folded and taped notepaper should have been easy to spot.

''How could our letters just disappear?''

He couldn't answer—and he didn't care. For the first time since he'd met Gillian, for the first time in his life, he knew one essential answer, the answer to what they were going to do.

He wove his fingers through hers and ushered her out of the tomb to the street. Hand in hand they raced through the quaint, narrow, rose-scented streets of Verona, past the shops, past the kiosks, past the Arena and the town square and the throngs of pedestrians smiling at them and nodding and thinking, *There go two happy lovers.* He raced with her back to the room behind the kitchen, to the narrow bed by the window.

And there, in the warm, rosy light of early evening, he told her, in a million different ways, how much he loved her.

Epilogue

In Juliet's possession, the two notes—one on a sheet of lined notepaper and the other on a leaf of hotel stationery—dissolved into glittering dust in her hands. "They need my help no more," she said.

Romeo heard the smug undertone in her voice, but did not chastise her for it. She had earned this success. She deserved to gloat.

"I would call this a happy ending," he said.

"The happiest," she crowed. "Look at them: not only have they found their love, but they no longer have to hide it in the night. They love each other even while the sun still hangs in the sky."

Romeo felt voyeuristic gazing down upon the two passionate bodies entwined in love and illuminated by the pearl pink light of a summer's evening sky. Yet ever since his death, he and Juliet had been voyeurs, watching the world below, the struggle and strife of lovers and haters, the excruciating joy of a love gone right and the sorrow of love gone wrong. They lived vicariously through the earth's lovers. They cheered when love triumphed and grieved when love failed.

What Romeo observed right now was the sweetest of triumphs. Gillian was utterly beautiful—not as beauti-

ful as his Juliet, but then, no woman could ever seem to him as beautiful as the woman he loved. And surely no woman could seem as beautiful to Owen as his Gillian. Her body was strong and ripe, her skin as soft and golden as the skin of a peach, her hair a celebration of primitive, natural freedom. Her breasts were gloriously round, swelling into Owen's powerful hands, his touch inflaming himself as well as his woman. She slid her legs along his and he groaned. Romeo could feel Owen's agonizing pleasure as if it were his own.

The lovers moved as one, their hearts and bodies following one rhythm, one thought, one single quest for their own happy ending. And in a shimmering moment of perfect unity they found it, exulted in it, cried out when their ecstasy became too great to contain.

"Ah, Juliet." Romeo sighed in admiration of his clever, generous wife. "You have said that anything is possible if there is enough love. Your wisdom has been rewarded."

"My lovers have been rewarded," she agreed, her eyes glittering like the remains of Owen's and Gillian's letters, still cupped in her palms. "The world has been rewarded. Would that there were only happy endings, we would know no more of war or loss or misery."

"There can never be only happy endings," he cautioned. "The world is not as good as you would wish it to be."

"But every happy ending makes it a little bit better. This happy ending—" she gestured to the contented lovers below "—makes it a great deal better. One success may lead to others, Romeo. Perhaps another happy ending shall have its beginning tomorrow."

"You are a dreamer," he murmured.

Juliet smiled. "We are both dreamers, my love. And sometimes dreams come true."

She lowered her gaze to Owen and Gillian, where they lay on the soft, wrinkled bed linens, their legs still intertwined. Gillian's hair was splayed out across Owen's chest and his arm was curved around her shoulders, sheltering her body. Gillian lifted her head until her eyes met Owen's, until her smile touched his.

Juliet opened her hands and released the stardust that had once been their plaintive letters, their written pleas for help, for love. The dust fell in a bright, sparkling shower down onto Gillian and Owen, lighting up the world.